Breathe Free

Nina Jones

SRL Publishing Ltd

SRL Publishing Ltd
Office 47396, PO Box 6945
London
W1A 6US

First published worldwide by SRL Publishing in 2021

ISBN: 978-1-9163373-7-4

This book is a work of fiction. Names, characters, places and
incidents are either a product of the author's imagination or are used
fictitiously. Any resemblance to actual people, living or dead, events
or locales, is entirely coincidental.

Chapter 1

4pm

I was running away from my first kiss. It was with Ryan
Sanders, and it was horrible. I didn't want to do it, but I
had to, for the girl I thought was my best friend: Misha. I
was running away from her, too.

My little brother Jake was running alongside me. The
grass was up to his knees, thrashing against his jeans. I
knew he was struggling to keep up but I had to get away
from them. I wouldn't slow down. Not yet.

When I pictured what my first kiss would be like, I
never thought I'd be able to see Jake wrinkling his nose
up in disgust, just behind the boy I was kissing. That boy
would never, ever, have been Ryan Sanders, either. I
wouldn't change it, though. That was the start of this
whole thing. If we hadn't run away up the fields, past the
point we promised not to cross, I'd never have met Anya.

I could hear Jake calling after me as I ran between
the first of the trees, near the edge of the Worker Camp.
I looked back, impatient, gesturing for him to hurry up.

'Nobody is chasing us!' he shouted.

I slowed down as the yard came into view, lingering
at the border between the trees and the grass. The facility
had always been just another grey building on the hill, but
we never knew there was a yard. It was hidden behind a
copse of trees in a dip at its edge, like a moat. Through
the other side, where I stood, there was just a few feet of

grass before the fence. I couldn't start the walk across it, somehow. Jake hung back with me, waiting.

The sun was going down, casting long shadows from the trees. I followed their sinewy arms, stretching across the grass to the other side. They grasped at a patch of grass behind the railings, that separated them from the concrete. There was a group of kids, playing football with a plastic bottle, laughing.

A girl stood in the goal. She had beautiful deep brown hair. It was almost black, but not quite. That was the first thing I noticed about her. It was flung forwards over her right shoulder and reached down to her waist in a plait, which meant it must have been even longer loose. It was like a silk rope. She was laughing. I watched her dive to the floor after the bottle as it skidded past her.

I thought they would be wearing some kind of uniform. Prison scrubs or something like that. They weren't. The girl I was watching had a red cardigan, blue jeans and a white t-shirt. She looked up and saw me. She smiled. I smiled back. I forgot about Ryan, Misha, Tom. The double-date we were supposed to go on. I forgot about her eyeliner and his aftershave. All that was in my head was the girl with the plait, smiling at me.

'Do you think they'll let us join in their game?' asked Jake.

I looked at the railings. They were easily twice my height, crowned with coils of barbed wire, like a lethal slinky.

'I don't think we can,' I said. I waved at the girl with the plait. She waved back.

'Who's that?' Jake asked.

'I don't know. Let's find out.'

Two hours earlier...

'Why does Jake have to come with us?' asked Misha. She was taking selfies, from different angles, to assess her new eyeliner. She had her hair pulled high and tight into a ponytail, with a clip-in extension piece that made it look as though she had a torrent of silky dark waves flowing from the top of her head down to the middle of her back. Her lipstick was neon pink. She could carry it off.

'Because mum wants him out of the house,' I replied, 'I can't do anything about it. I'm sorry,' she sighed.

'It's shit, this one. Just smudges. Leaves crumbly bits like it's a flaky mascara. It's not even mascara. I don't get it.'

'What time did you say we'd meet them?' I asked, looking at my face in my phone's camera. She'd tried out her new contouring kit on me earlier. I knew I looked horrendous, despite what she said. I kept trying to rub it away with my sleeve when she wasn't looking.

'Stop that!' she said, pulling my hand away.

'Sorry.'

'Okay,' she said, flicking her phone screen off and looking at me, 'we need to talk tactics. Remember what we said? If he likes me, make yourself and -' she rolled her eyes, '-*Jake* - scarce. Yeah?'

I nodded. I wanted to say, *what if he likes me?* But I would never have dared. It wasn't worth the grief. Besides, I knew he never would, because when Misha had asked him to rank all the girls on our row in science just the day before, he put me last. *He's horrible. She's horrible, sometimes. Why are you doing this?*

'Don't leave me, though, if he's being a dick, yeah? You know what he's like,' she flicked her mirror back on and smoothed her eyebrows into place.

'I won't.'

'Smile!' she said, putting her hand on my shoulder,

3

'you might finally get off with someone! His mate's quite fit, you know. I mean, there's the B.O. thing, sure, but anyone can learn to use deodorant. He has good hair. And he *definitely* fancies you.'

'I'm just going to get Jake,' I said, checking the time on my phone and counting how many hours until we'd be back.

***

Ryan had doused himself in something so strong it made my eyes water when the breeze caught him in front of me. I was struggling to play my part. Especially with Jake there. I felt bad, ignoring him. Being irritated with him. He didn't want to be there either. It was a beautiful afternoon, too. The sun was out, but there was a breeze. The light was gold. *I should be lying in the grass, reading a book. Or having a water fight with Jake. Not standing here listening to Ryan bore on about bikes and the fact he can't unlock the next level on that game.* I leaned against a tree and picked at its bark, watching him, pretending to be interested in what he was saying.

'So anyway,' he carried on, 'that's why I was wondering if you wanted to come see *Stealth* next week.'

Shit. I wasn't listening.

'What, with Misha and Tom?'

'Yeah. Like a double-date sort of thing.'

Quick, think.

'Hang on, I think Jake's got stuck,' I said, pointing vaguely in his direction.

I left Ryan and ran over to the tree Jake was starting to climb. He didn't need my help.

'Can we go yet?' he asked, jumping down to the floor.

I sighed and looked over at Misha. She was sitting

on the grass with Tom, periodically tugging at the hem of her skirt to make sure her knickers weren't showing. She shot me a glance. Ryan was watching me. He looked hurt.

'Not yet. Come on. Let's play hide-and-seek. Ryan can join in. Shall we hide...so well, that he'll never find us?'

'Yeah!'

We ran over to him. Misha was still glaring at me. 'Let's play hide-and-seek with Jake,' I said to Ryan.

'Okay,' he smiled.

I was surprised at how enthusiastic he seemed. I felt her eyes burning into me still.

'Hang on, I just need a word with Misha,' I said to Jake, 'wait there.'

I walked over to Misha and Tom. They were watching something on her phone. She looked up.

'Have you seen this?' she asked me, 'it's hilarious. Tom's dog. So cute.'

'Can I have a word?' I asked.

'Back in a min,' she said to him, getting up, holding her skirt in place.

'Why did you run off from him?' she asked, as we walked into the longer grass. She took the opportunity to check her face in her mirror and apply some more perfume.

'I just had to check on Jake,' I lied, 'he's bored. How's it going? Do you want me to go? Or hang around?'

'It's going good actually. But don't go - stay. It would really help me out if you could get off with Ryan. If Tom sees you two doing that, he might decide to finally kiss me.'

'No. I really don't-'

'Christ, Emma, you're such a *baby*. It's not like you're going to have *sex* with him. It's a kiss. He's fit. Just try not to breathe through your nose.'

'Fine. For god's sake, Misha.'

'What? I let you bring Jake, didn't I? Plus, I did your contouring. You owe me.'

'Just tell me when we can go home,' I called back to her as I walked back to them.

I heard her mutter something behind me. I rolled my eyes.

'Finally,' said Ryan as I finished my step-dragging meander back to where he stood. I sighed.

'Right,' Ryan announced, 'Jake, you need to close your eyes and count to, I don't know…100. Me and Emma will go hide somewhere and-'

'No,' I interrupted, 'me and Jake are hiding from *you.*'

'Oh. Wait - what? But then we get to hide after, right?' he asked.

I was watching Misha. She made a *hurry up* gesture with her hands, mouthing *come on* at me while Tom scrolled through his timeline.

Jesus Christ.

'Fine, yeah. Whatever,' I said to Ryan, then turned to Jake. 'Hang on, there's just something I have to do.' He watched me.

I took a deep breath. *Just get it over with.*

'Do you want to kiss me?' I asked Ryan.

'What?'

'Do you want to kiss me,' I repeated, this time as a statement rather than a question.

'What - you mean, here? Now?'

'Yep.'

'Oh. Well, erm-'

'Don't worry, it's fine,' I turned and held my hand out, 'come on Jake, let's go home.'

'No, wait! I do. It's just,' he cleared his throat and

6

glanced down at the floor, then back up to me. 'I've never kissed anyone before.'

It made me feel a bit better. I thought I was the only kid left in our year that hadn't.

'Don't worry, I haven't either.'

I stood there and watched him step closer.

Don't breathe through your nose. Don't breathe through your nose. That was stupid advice. It meant I couldn't breathe at all once he started. I had to give in and smell the aftershave-over-unwashed-sweat in the end. His breath wasn't bad, so that was something at least. He kept changing position, as though he was trying to find a way to create a perfectly airtight seal around my mouth. It felt weird. Wet. I tried not to gag when he tentatively touched my tongue with his. It didn't feel like we were doing it right.

'Eurgh!' I heard Jake say.

Ryan had his eyes closed. I tried to see past his massive face to look at Misha. She did a thumbs-up gesture and mouthed *thank you*.

I waited, giving her some time. Ryan put his hand on my bum. I took it off. When I looked again, Misha was kissing Tom. *Thank god.*

'Right,' I said, pulling away, 'come on Jake, let's hide.'

'You're disgusting!' Jake said.

'I know. Start counting, Ryan.' I wiped my sleeve over my mouth to get rid of his saliva. I looked at him. He was blushing. 'Ryan?'

'Sorry,' he said, shaking his head, 'I'll count.'

He closed his eyes and covered them, like a child, then started counting.

'Come on,' I grabbed Jake's hand. 'Let's go.'

4pm

'Is this place why we're not allowed up here?' Jake asked, as we stepped towards the railings. We were both still out of breath from running. I smoothed my hair back as best as I could, behind my ears, and straightened my t-shirt. The girl with the plait walked over.

'Maybe,' I answered him, 'but mum will never find out. Look, someone's coming to say hi. I bet they're bored, here. Let's keep them company for a bit.'

Chapter 2

Two months later...

'Anya - what do you think?'

'Of what?'

'This, look.'

I turned the sketch pad round so she could see it through the bars.

'Wow, did you just draw that?'

I nodded. I thought it was a bit rubbish. Maybe she was humouring me. It was supposed to be a sketch of her, with the facility behind.

She reached her hand through the bars. 'Can I?' she asked.

'Oh, sure, you can have it.'

I tore the page out and posted it through the railings. She took it and scanned her eyes over the page.

'Hang on,' she said, 'you need to sign it. And date it.'

I laughed.

'No, I'm serious!'

She fed it back through. I leaned the paper against the pad and signed it, with the date underneath, shaking my head.

'Ridiculous,' I said, giving it back.

'I don't know when I'll be moved,' she said, 'I need something to remember you by.'

'What?' I asked, looking up as I put my pencil case back in my bag.

'We get moved on, all the time. Depends on where the work is. I think this contract is for a couple of years, but sometimes they end early. Sometimes they move you to a new contract before, anyway. Just because they decide they need you more, somewhere else.'

'But... I thought kids didn't have to move?'

'Why? What's the difference between me and a seventeen-year-old? It's not like we get to go to school or anything. The only difference is if you have a family. If my parents were here, I'd go wherever they went. That's the only difference. But they're not.'

She traced her finger over the face in the drawing. 'It's really good, this. It's like you've known me for longer. Like you know my family, too. I have my mum's eyes, my dad's nose, my grandma's mouth,' she said, smiling.

I skipped past Anya's comment about her family, because the week before she'd finally told me what happened to them, and I wanted to forget.

'They're supposed to give you some kind of school here though, aren't they?' I asked.

She shrugged. 'I don't know. The ones who need it get some English. I think the kids under twelve get Worker Education classes, but I don't really know what that is.'

She shrugged again, putting the paper on the grass, then she turned around and picked up a book behind her. 'I'm okay, though,' she said, 'because I have you!' she smiled, holding up my textbook.

'Wow,' I said, 'I thought you just wanted them because you were bored. I didn't think it was all you had...' I thought of all the textbooks I had, that I ignored, at home.

'They're good,' she said, 'I'm lucky. I hide them. They'd get stolen if the other kids knew. Or confiscated

10

if the guards found them.'

'Can't you leave the Scheme, somehow? There must be a way…you should be at school, with me,' I said, 'you could come and live at my house, there's no reason why not-'

'Emma, do you know what you're saying? It's madness,' she said, shaking her head. 'Look, give me your phone.'

I passed it through the bars. She scrolled and tapped. I watched her eyes looking down at the phone. Her eyelids were a perfect almond, fringed with eyelashes that Misha would kill for. She lifted the phone and flipped it round, so that the screen faced me. It was a video from one of the charity accounts I followed.

'Look,' she said, pointing to the screen, 'that's what happens if you run away.'

Grainy footage of a chain-link fence filled the screen. The camera pulled back showing a couple with a child, waiting by the fence. The woman was holding the boy in her arms. He was maybe about three or four. Just younger than Jake. They were watching a line of trees, not far away from the fence. It was exactly like where we were sitting, only the hills on the horizon were higher, rockier, drier. I couldn't tell if it was early morning or early evening - the light was either just coming up or just falling.

Someone emerged from between the trees and waved to them. They looked around, then the man peeled the chain-link back. It must have been hacked open already. The woman bent down, gripping the child as she made her way through the gap to the other side. The man followed, replacing the fence behind them. They looked around again, then ran towards the trees.

One alarm started screaming, then another. I couldn't see their faces anymore, just the back of them, as they ran faster towards the trees. The child looked back at the fence, then at us. He was crying. There was shouting. The camera panned over to the left, where three men ran out of the building, across the yard and through the hole in the fence. They had guns. The family were nearly at the trees. They shot one last look back, then disappeared into the woods.

'They made it!' I said, finally daring to breathe.

Anya shook her head. I heard a shot and looked down at the video. The men were stood just in front of the trees, peering through the sights of their guns and firing, one after the other.

Five shots in total.

I didn't want to carry on watching. I handed her the phone back. I didn't want to speak because I knew I'd sob.

'You think that won't happen here?' she asked.

I couldn't answer. I shook my head.

'You think that stuff only happens on the other side of the world - not here? That was filmed in Italy. It's only a matter of time. The security here have guns. Just because they haven't used them yet, doesn't mean they won't.'

'Why did the alarms go off?' I managed, sniffing, trying to hold it back.

Anya uncrossed her legs and thrust her foot towards the railings as she pulled up the leg of her jeans.

'This,' she said, pointing to the grey plastic cuff around her ankle. One red light blinked at me from a raised panel directly above her ankle joint.

Jake was the first one to spot them, the first time we met the kids. I remember him asking why they all had bracelets on their ankles. I asked Anya. She said it was to keep track of them. Towards the end of her yard time, a little red light always started flashing. Once, she stayed a little too long, and it began beeping.

'If you go beyond the border, it triggers an alarm,' she said, 'all the countries in the scheme have them.' She crossed her legs again.

'What do you need?' I asked, trying to swallow the last of the tears and compose myself. She looked at me. 'To learn, I mean,' I said, 'books. Pens. Calculators, whatever. I'll try to get it. Anything - just give me a list and I'll see what I can get hold of.'

'Toothpaste,' she said, 'my tooth hurts so much. Please, please get me some toothpaste.'

***

I visited Anya every week, sometimes every day, for months. I lied to Misha. I had to. There was no way she'd understand. No way she'd let me. I told her my parents had become obsessed with my grades, and they'd decided I needed after school tuition so that I could pass the scholarship test for the private school sixth form.

Misha was so angry about it. She told me I was being selfish, because it meant we didn't see each other every day anymore. She said I was vain to think I could get into the good school. People like us couldn't do that. She wouldn't be going there, so how could I think of leaving her? I wanted to tell her I'd been desperate to leave her for years. I didn't, though, of course I didn't. I just lied, like I always did.

I said my parents didn't want anyone knowing in case I failed, to save them the embarrassment. I knew Misha would tell her parents anyway, but at least this way they might feel too awkward to quiz mine about it.

I started to worry that I might be in love with Anya, after a while. I couldn't wait to see her. I could never concentrate in school because it all seemed so irrelevant.

I just wanted to be with her, talking about silly little things, or big important things, or nothing at all – just sitting in silence while we read magazines or worked through whatever textbook she wanted to focus on that week.

She was the most beautiful person I'd ever met, too. I think she caught me, sometimes, staring at her. She would laugh and ask me what I was looking at. I never had an answer.

I decided it was love, but it wasn't *that* kind of love. I was in awe of her, for certain. But she gave me something no-one else ever had – she made me feel good about myself. *Maybe this is what real friendship is like*, I thought. Someone who listens to you, cares about you, roots for you.

I was so scared of her leaving. I knew she could, any time, with no notice. Every time the kids poured out of the door into the yard, I'd have to pull myself back from the verge of a panic attack, convinced she'd been moved, until she appeared.

That day, she was the last one out. I was sweating, gripping the railings. She finally emerged and bounded over, grinning as though she hadn't nearly made me black-out.

I took a deep breath. 'I have a plan,' I said, 'to help the kids in here. Maybe even get you out of here one day.'

Her smile fell. I took an old mobile out of my pocket and told her my idea. She was quiet for too long.

'You don't have to do this,' she said, finally.

'No, it's a good idea. I think it will help, honestly.' She took the phone, reluctantly.

'It's the only way to prove what it's like in there, right?' I asked.

'I'm not saying it's not a good idea, it's just…

dangerous.'

I didn't have an answer for that. It was easy for me to say it was the right thing to do. I wasn't the one having to do it.

'Where did you get it from?' she asked, turning it over in her hands.

'It's just my mum's old one. It's on pay-as-you-go. She's on a new contract. I can keep topping this one up.'

'If they find it, they'll trace it back to you, you know?'

I shrugged. 'They see us talking nearly every day when you get your yard time. They can't think I'm a threat. I mean, I'm not, I'm a fourteen-year-old girl. They'd have told me to go by now surely.'

'Still, I don't like bringing your family into this.'

'Look, if they take it off you just be honest. To a point. Tell them I gave you a phone because I wanted to keep in touch with you. That's all.'

'They'll find the films though, if I do manage to get any. It will be obvious that I'm using the phone to gather evidence,' she said, glancing around her.

'So? They can't do anything to you just for trying to improve things in there.'

Anya laughed, shaking her head. 'Emma, you're so naïve. Things aren't the same for us in here, as they are for you out there. Just remember that.'

She handed the phone back through the bars. I wouldn't take it. 'Emma. I'll just drop it on the grass if you don't take it. It's not worth it.'

'Not worth it? Your life? The lives of all those people in there with you?'

She dropped the phone on my side. Her face changed. 'You have no idea what you're talking about, Emma,' she said, quiet anger simmering under her voice. 'You have no idea how things work in there. Or what we have to go through. Don't talk to me about the value of *my life*. The value of *theirs*,' she said, pointing to the kids playing behind her. 'You can't play your *saving the world game* with our lives. You go home at night to a family, a warm house, food, freedom. You go to school. Get an education. You decide where you go, and when. When you're old enough you can leave home and go wherever you want. Do whatever you want. We have none of that.'

Her anklet started flashing. We both looked at it.

'You think I'm scared of being told off by someone?' she asked, 'as though it's just a teacher who will keep me behind after school? You think I just don't want to cause a scene? Just think about what happened to my family before you judge me. Think about the family you saw on that video, the ones who were shot in the woods. Think about what it's like to live in there,' she pointed to the building behind her, 'or wherever they tell you to live, never knowing how long you'll be there for, what job you'll be put on, who you'll be sold to next. Knowing that one step out of line could land you somewhere worse. Or dead. You're ignorant, Emma. Arrogant, too.'

Her anklet beeped. I couldn't talk. I was crying. She had tears in her eyes but they wouldn't fall. As though her rage was so strong it stopped gravity.

'Keep your phone,' she said through her teeth, then turned and walked back inside.

***

Just go and say you're sorry, I told myself. *You can't let this ruin everything. You can still help her. Somehow.*

I knew I couldn't.

I tortured myself, thinking she'd be gone, she'd have left, by the time I went back. *How will you live with yourself?*

When I saw her there, waiting by the railings, I

16

exhaled and looked up at the sky thanking someone, something.

She smiled when she saw me, but there was something different in it. Something sad. I wanted to hug her.

'I'm sorry,' I said, stopping just in front of the railings.

She reached her hand through the bars and I held it. She gave her head the slightest, gentlest shake. We said nothing for a while - just stood, holding our hands through the railings looking at each other.

'Come on,' she said, 'let me do your hair.'

I laughed.

She had an hour that day. Once a week they got a whole hour of yard time. Sometimes we watched an episode of something on my phone, or I'd try to repeat a lesson I'd had that week in school for her, or we'd sit and write out our grand plans for what we'd do if we lived in New America.

'I still feel bad,' she said, her voice so close behind me, 'about the things I said.'

I felt shivers across my scalp and shoulder blades as she separated my hair into three sections. I was backed up as close to the bars as I could get, so she could reach her fingers through and plait my hair just like hers.

I loved being a kid with Anya. I did *kid* things when I was with Jake, of course, but this was different. I wasn't acting younger than I was, like I had to with Jake, or older than I was like I had to with Misha. I was just me.

'Stop apologising. I'm the one who should keep saying sorry. You were right. I *am* ignorant. And it was arrogant of me to think-'

'No, it wasn't,' she interrupted me, still weaving my hair together. 'You were just trying to help. You want to make things better. I shouldn't have thrown it back at you like that. I wasn't angry with *you*. I was angry with *them*. With the world, for letting this happen. There,' she said, holding a hand over my shoulder for me to pass her a hairband, 'you're d-'

'Emma?' a voice interrupted.

Shit. Misha.

She was walking with Tom and a few of his friends. They had a bottle of vodka they were taking turns to swig from. First she looked confused, then disgusted.

'What the hell are you doing?' she said, stopping right in front of us more or less looking down her nose at me. I stood up.

'This is Anya,' I said, 'she's one of the-'

'Yeah I know what she is,' she said, giving her a sideways glance. 'I'm asking what the hell you're doing here. It's dangerous.'

Tom and his friends crowded around the railings to our left, looking at the kids on the other side. The kids ignored them. Anya told me that most of them had learned not to go near anyone who came too close. If anyone did venture this far up the fields to the back of the camp, it was usually to throw things, or shout things, or just stare at them.

'Why are you all here?' I asked, watching them.

'We're on our way to Tolly's party in the wood,' Tom pointed to the trees just past the camp, 'you want to come? There's a ton of booze.'

Misha's eyes narrowed.

'Was she doing your hair?' she laughed. 'Jesus. Are you eight years old?'

'Is this Misha?' Anya asked.

'Yep that's me,' Misha said stepping forwards.

Shit. Don't.

'Makes sense,' said Anya with a slight nod.

'What do you mean by that?' Misha said, her voice

18

brittle.

'Don't start, Misha,' I said.

'What? *She* started it. Look, are you coming with us or what?' she asked, turning away from Anya. I knew she didn't want me at the party. She didn't want Tom to talk to me. But she didn't want me here either.

'Emma,' she lowered her voice, 'it's dangerous here. Do you know anything about her? Why she's here or who she knows or-'

'I'll see you tomorrow, Misha, I'm not coming to Tolly's party. I'm going home. I have a headache.'

'Okay,' she murmured, turning to eye Anya again, 'long as you're not staying here. It's going dark soon.'

With a flick of her hair she set off and the boys followed. I shook my head, exhaling. I caught Anya smirking.

'What?'

'She can't walk in those shoes,' she said, pointing down the hill.

I hadn't even noticed. I looked back and saw her hobbling over the uneven ground in her heels.

'Are you going, then? Or should I finish your hair?' she asked.

I smiled and sat down, shuffling back up against the railings.

***

'Are you seriously telling me you're missing *my* birthday party?' Misha asked, folding her arms.

'Why are you missing her party?' Jake piped up.

We were walking home from school. She was already annoyed with me for detouring via Jake's school to pick him up. Mum's shift finished too late on Thursdays, so I always picked him up instead. Misha knew that, but still got in a mood about it every time. As though one week, to avoid her strop I'd just leave him there to find his own way home.

'She's seeing Anya,' Misha answered him.

'Unbelievable.'

'Ooh, are we seeing Anya this weekend?' Jake asked squeezing my hand, looking up at me.

'Thanks, Misha.' I sighed.

'Oh. I'm sorry, did I ruin your date? I can't *believe* you're putting her over me.'

'I'm not, Misha, it's just...they've cut down her yard time a lot recently and she finds out this week whether she's moving to-'

'Don't bother telling me,' she said, putting up a hand, 'because I really do find it all so boring, it makes me want to stick pins in my eyes.'

'Eurgh!' said Jake.

We walked on in silence.

'Seriously though, Emma,' she said after a while, 'I'm pissed off with you, yes, but I'm mainly just worried about you. Honestly. I've heard bad things about the people in that place. There's a reason they're in there, you know.'

'Come on, Jake,' I interrupted her, yanking Jake's hand so that he followed me in the other direction, 'we're getting the bus.'

'Fuck's sake, Emma,' she shouted after me, 'I'm not being racist or whatever it is you think I am. I'm your friend!'

I carried on walking, dragging Jake who was staring back at Misha.

'Or I *was*,' she called after me, 'until *she* came along!'

***

I watched Jake's eyelashes slowly fan down, then back up, as he tried to stay awake.

'I'll leave it there, until tomorrow,' I said, closing the book.

He murmured a protest.

'Come on, bedtime. Do you want me to get Daddy to draw you a picture for when you wake up again, when he gets back from work?'

Jake smiled and nodded.

'Okay. Night-night then.'

I hugged him and turned off the light.

'Emma?' he said as I was closing the door.

'Hm?'

'Can I come with you, on Saturday?'

I hesitated.

'Please?'

'Okay. But remember what I said okay? You can't tell Mum or Dad.'

'I won't.'

'Night.'

I closed the door and immediately regretted saying yes.

I could hear voices outside. Mum must have picked Dad up from the station on her way back. They were arguing as quietly as they could manage. I decided to stay on the landing, listening to the keys clank in the lock and their voices spill through into the hall.

'I'm not saying we *shouldn't* ground her,' Mum's hushed voice floated up. 'I'm just saying if we come down on her too hard, it might only make matters worse. She might hide all kinds of things from us. We need her to feel she can trust us.'

'Oh for god's sake. Don't-'

'One day it's this, the next it could be worse. Something illegal. Wouldn't you rather she told us?'

I rubbed my eyes. *Bollocks.* I sighed and made my way down the stairs. *Might as well get it over with.* They both looked up at me.

'Hello, love,' Mum said with a nervous smile.

'We need to have a word,' added Dad, 'come through.'

He walked into the kitchen. Mum smiled at me again. I took a deep breath and followed her in.

'Cup of tea?' Dad asked, filling up the kettle.

'No, thanks. You need to draw Jake something tonight, he asked for it. Dinosaurs, maybe. Or something with Monster Trucks.'

Dad nodded. I sat at the kitchen table. Mum sat opposite me, fidgeting. Dad leaned against the work surface, arms folded, waiting for the kettle to boil. He looked at mum.

'We've just been speaking to Misha's mum,' she said finally looking at me.

'Oh. And?'

Come on, get it over with.

'Why didn't you tell us?' Dad said pouring hot water into the empty mugs, *then* adding the tea bags. He knew it annoyed me when he did it that way around.

'We think it's great that you want to help, Emma,' said Mum, 'but there are better ways to do it.'

'Better causes,' muttered Dad.

'Well, he has a point there to be honest, love,' she agreed.

'I take it you're talking about my friend in the Worker Camp,' I said, impatient.

They winced.

'She's not your friend, Emma,' Mum said, sitting up straighter, 'you don't know her.'

'I can't believe you can get that close. It's dangerous.' Dad said, shaking his head.

'Why does everyone keep saying that? Do you think they have the plague or something? They're refugee children, they-'

'Two mistakes, there,' Dad cut in, 'one - it's not the children we're bothered about. It's the adults. And two, they're not refugees. They're Workers.'

I was so close to doing the thing I always do. Ranting at them. Shouting and storming off. It was Jangles, weirdly, who saved me. Just at that moment she wandered through the kitchen and started pawing at the cat flap.

'Use your tray, Jangles,' mum said to her, 'it's locked for a reason.'

Jangles looked at her.

'Why can't she go out?' I asked.

'She knows what she did,' Mum said giving her a sideways glance.

Jangles and I exchanged a knowing look. I decided to play the long game.

'Look,' I sighed, 'I'm sorry. I won't go there again.' Then I panicked that I was being suspiciously reasonable. 'I'm still going to that march, though. I don't care if you don't sign the thing for school. I'm doing the walkout.'

They looked at each other, trying to hide their smiles. Mum was smug because she thought her softly-softly approach had worked. Dad was impressed. He held his hands up.

'Fine, you win,' he said, 'go on the climate thing. I'll even sign the permission slip, so you don't get a detention.'

I walked over to the cat flap and unlocked it. Jangles shot out.

'Emma!' Mum protested.

'Oh, I'm sorry, I forgot,' I lied, hiding my smile.

Chapter 3

'Okay, I'm ready. Just pull it.'

'Are you sure?'

She nodded, closing her eyes.

'Hold on to the railings, then.'

I tried to concentrate on my breathing and steady my hands. Jake hovered behind me, watching Anya's face. He probably didn't think anything could go wrong. Or maybe that's exactly what he was waiting for.

'Come on!' squealed Jake, jigging with excitement.

'No! Shh!' I snapped back. 'Not until I say so.'

Anya held the railings. I can still see her skinny fingers, knuckles blanching tight round the grey steel. She squinted one of her eyes open, black and dense. The green garden twine dangling from her mouth started to tremble.

'Okay,' I took another deep breath and wrapped the other end round my palm until it made a taut line. The line quivered between my hand on my side of the steel railings, and her mouth on the other side. I decided to count her down. I could feel Jake behind me. I knew the look on his face without turning around. Eyes so big they threatened to erupt from their sockets.

'3…'

Anya closed the squinting eye.

'2…'

Her fingers braced.

'1!' I wrenched as hard as I could. Anya screamed. Jake let out a cry of delight. The twine snapped back almost instantly - I thought it had slipped off the tooth and we'd have to do it again. Then I saw Anya on the floor.

'She's dead! You killed her! Emmy, you killed her!' Jake shouted as he rushed over to the railings. I faltered forwards and peered between the grey steel bars. I felt like all the blood left my insides to thrash across my face and temples or thud in my ears.

There was the tooth, just by her feet, like a white insect larva just wrenched from a corpse it was gestating in, smeared in bright blood. My legs started to crumple under me.

'Anya!' I shouted.

Her face had changed from almond-shell to sail-sheet. Blood seeped from her lip, slowly, down to the grass under her cheek.

'Anya, wake up!'

I spun round, fell to my knees to dig through the rucksack and find the bottle of saltwater I'd packed.

'Are you alright?' I heard Jake whisper. I looked round.

'Anya!'

She blinked and put one hand to her face, pushing herself up off the grass with the other. She frowned, opening her mouth to prod at the wound. More blood spilled out.

'Yuck!' shouted Jake.

'Shut up, Jake. Here, Anya, swish around your mouth with this then spit it out. It'll help the infection.'

I took the lid off and squeezed it enough for it to pass between the bars. Reaching my arm through as far as I could, to the shoulder, I waited for her fingers to reach mine and take it from me. Her hand was hot.

'Don't drink it,' Jake said. 'Saltwater makes you go mad, then it kills you.'

Anya nodded silently, taking a swig. She started to swish but stopped suddenly, screwing up her face and making a shrieking hum before turning and spitting a jet of goop over the grass. Thick yellow, streaked with red. She stared at it, gagging.

'Better out than in,' I said, hopefully. 'If you keep it clean now, you should be okay.'

'Thank you.'

Her fingers crept across the grass to the tooth. She picked it up and wiped it with her sleeve.

'Are you keeping it?' I asked.

She nodded, wiping the blood off it. 'I think I can get something for this.'

A shrill electronic sound cut through our tooth-jewel gazing. Anya looked at her ankle. The cuff flashed and chirped. She sighed. I dug in the rucksack again, handing her fistfuls of stolen treasure through the railings - sachets of salt and sugar from the cafe on our corner, a bar of soap from my mum's drawer, plasters from the first-aid kit in the kitchen, the stubby pencil we keep for writing notes to stick on the fridge. She took them from me and passed the empty plastic bottle back.

'Use the salt for your mouth,' I said. 'I'll bring more next time.'

She stuffed the items up her red cardigan sleeves and smiled.

'I'll bring you something next time, too. I'm on fruit-picking Thursday.'

'Yay!' Jake cried, 'can you get us those things that look like aliens?'

She nodded, laughing.

26

'Don't, Anya, it's too dangerous,' I said, frowning at Jake.

The bleeps sounded from her ankle again. She kissed her hand and blew it across to Jake, then me, before turning and running across the grass and over the yard to the door. I picked up the twine and reeled it in, winding it round my hand.

'Why are you so mean to me when we see Anya?' Jake asked, watching his feet stomp down the hill as we walked back towards the house.

'I'm not mean, I'm just being firm. I have to be firm because it's dangerous. You have to behave, otherwise you can't come with me.'

I saw the pouting lip start to tremble.

'Look,' I stopped, putting my hand on his shoulder, 'I'm sorry. Anya is our friend. We have to look after her. You're my little brother, I have to look after *you*. I'm sure Anya will bring you some of the alien fruit when we see her next.'

'So I can come with you next time?' he said, sniffing. I nodded.

'Anyway. You haven't shown me how fast you can run for a while. Last one to the back gate does the dishes tonight,' I said, speeding up. He laughed and ran ahead.

***

If mum hadn't chopped onion that night, things might've turned out differently.

'Where have all the plasters gone?' she asked, frowning at the empty pocket in the green canvas bag. She was still in her cashier uniform, the cut in her fingertip threatening to spill blood on the orange polyester.

I tried to catch Jake's eye to stare into his soul, in a

bid to stop him answering.

'Emmy took them,' he said, without looking up.

I kicked Jake under the table. Mum looked at me. He looked up, suddenly realising, mouthing *sorry*.

'I took them to school…' I started but couldn't think of a reason quick enough.

'Why?'

'It was homework,' Jake offered.

Shit.

'Have you been up to the Camp again?' Mum folded her arms, fixing me with a steady stare.

'Why do they call it a *camp* when there's nobody camping there? It's just a big prison. There aren't any tents or anything,' Jake said.

I let his question hang in the air.

'Emma, have you been there again?' Mum repeated.

'No…'

'You know it's not safe there, Emma,' she said, pointing out of the window, then at me, 'you promised me…'

'Anya's our friend and we have to look after her,' Jake interrupted, with an earnest nod. I gripped the outer edges of my chair. *Fuck.*

'*What?* You took Jake there, too? Right,' she slammed the cupboard door shut, 'you're not leaving the house without me for the next two weeks, Emma. I'll pick you up and drop you off at school. I would've thought you could be trusted to walk to school by yourself at your age, but here we are. I'm so disappointed in you. After you *promised* me,' she shook her head, looking out of the window, then back at me, 'they're there for a *reason*, Emma. It's not our decision what happens to them and neither is it any of our business. What do you think you're achieving?'

I stared at the grain of the wooden table. I couldn't

answer her question even if I'd wanted to. I didn't know what I was trying to do. I just felt that what was happening was wrong, and if I could just help one person, then it was better than nothing. I wish I'd said that to her.

'Your dad is going to be so angry about this. Endangering Jake, too. For what?'

'It's not dangerous, mum- *they're* the ones in danger.'

As soon as the words came out, I wished I could cram them back in.

'Are you serious?' Mum put her hands over her face. She rubbed her eyes then dragged her fingers down over her cheeks. 'My god, Emma. I can't believe how naïve you are sometimes. They are getting paid to work. They have everything they need. They knew what they were getting into when they came here. Half of them are murderers, rapists, violent criminals who-'

'They're not! You don't know what you're talking about, Mum.'

'They *are*,' Mum hissed, her voice taking on that quiet rage I dreaded, 'you just ask your dad. He didn't find them so pleasant when they stole his car at knifepoint! Why would they be locked up if they were harmless? Why would Border Patrol have guns? Hm?'

I knew there was no point arguing. I got up to leave.

'You're not going out,' she said, blocking the doorway.

'I'm going to my room.'

She stepped aside.

'That boy who helped in the escape,' she shouted up the stairs after me, 'the police have him now. Emma! Are you listening? Their dogs bit his arm so badly-' I slammed my door, '-he might lose it!' she trailed off.

***

29

'Are we going to see Anya?' Jake asked, hanging upside-down off the top bunk. His pyjama top had fallen down to his neck, his ribs casting shadow lines over his chest. His hair stretched straight like the bristles of a broom.

'I might be. But you can't come.'

He bent up and hauled himself onto the bunk.

'Why? Emmy, you promised to be nice to me.'

'No I didn't, I promised to *look after* you.'

'But she'll have the alien fruit now... yesterday was Thursday.'

'I'll bring it back for you.'

He fell silent, fiddling with the elastic on his sock. I looked out of the window.

'Do you think Benji would've liked her?' he asked.

'Who?'

'Anya.'

'Yeah,' I smiled, 'he would've.'

'I think he would have liked the alien fruit, too.'

I nodded.

'You know that's why Mum is angry with you, don't you?' Jake said quietly, looking up.

I looked at him.

'She's worried because of what happened to Benji,' he continued, 'she doesn't-'

'Benji was very poorly,' I interrupted, 'he never went near the camp.' Still, I knew exactly what he meant.

'How are you going to get out to see her?' he asked.

'I don't know, now they're both watching me all the time... but I have to try. Anyway,' I said, getting up and switching his nightlight on, 'you were supposed to be in bed half an hour ago and I was supposed to be reading you a story.'

When I got back to my room, I put my forehead to

the window and looked down. It was a long way to the concrete flags. There was a drainpipe to one side of my window, running down to the ground, but it looked plastic and flimsy. Light shone out from the living room onto the lawn, which meant they were still watching TV. Above the bay window of the living room, though, there was a small, flat roof. Above, that, just close enough to make a jump possible, Mum and Dad's bedroom window. I nodded to myself.

I took out a piece of paper and a pen from my drawer and started to scribble.

Anya,

I can't come to see you when I said I would, I've been grounded. I can only come at night for the next week or so, until I'm allowed out, so I probably won't see you. In the meantime, here are some bits that you might like. I'll see you soon.

Love,
Emmy

I paused, then added *and Jake.*

I listened on the landing. The gentle buzz of the TV was there, but I couldn't hear anything else. I held my breath, leaning over the banister. A loud yawn startled me backwards. I made out some words - *after this* - and concluded they wouldn't be coming up until after the programme finished.

I knew where the creaky floorboards were in their room and managed to avoid them. The old wooden window frame with its rusty metal latch was so loud. The only way to open it silently was by holding everything so tight and moving so slow that the joints in my fingers ached. Finally the night air rushed in through the window, fresh on my flushed face. All I had for Anya was a pen, some socks and a chocolate bar. I managed to cram it all in the zip-pocket of my hoodie.

I sat on the windowsill and swung my legs over the edge, out into the night. I took a deep breath and looked down, telling myself it wasn't far. I pushed up with my hands either side of me and lowered my body down as far as I could, my tiptoes just reaching the flat ledge of the roof under me. I had to let go. The back of my heels slammed down and I winced at the sound, listening for any reaction from the living room. The TV carried on. I couldn't hear any movement. Now I could see the flaw in my plan. The only way off the roof was to scale down the window - the window of the room my parents were sat in, with the curtains open. *Shit.*

Shit shit shit.

I heard mum's voice get closer. She was walking to the window, saying something about the cat. I heard a dragging, rolling sound and realised she was closing the curtains, as the light on the lawn disappeared. I exhaled in the darkness, turned around on my hands and knees and lowered myself down, clinging to the guttering. I stepped down the edge of the frame until I could balance my feet on the ledge.

Now I was stuck. I couldn't let go without falling backwards, but I couldn't get down without letting go. I was going to have to jump - to try to turn and jump all in one go, onto the lawn. The guttering creaked in my hands. I tried to shuffle my feet so they were pointing towards the lawn and turn my body that way, too.

Slowly, I took one hand off the guttering. As soon as I took it away, I knew my balance had gone. I tried to power my fall forwards by leaning towards the grass as my feet went from under me but I fell sideways, heavy, into the planters that lined the path down the side of the

32

house.

Shit. I stumbled to my feet, half covered in soil. The pain rang through one side, my ribs and shoulder on fire, my teeth rattled in their roots.

'EMMA! What the HELL are you doing?' Dad shouted, storming up the path. I turned to run but crumpled with the pain. He grabbed my arm before I could take a step and dragged me back, towards the house.

As we turned the corner, I screwed up the note from my pocket and threw it down the side of the garage.

***

'Are you not even going to let me take Jake to Sam's birthday party?' I asked, knowing the answer.

'No. You're grounded. You know you're grounded, so stop asking,' Mum snapped. She had that tone in her voice. The tone of exasperation. Irritation. The tone that used to make me worry that she actually hated me. That was before I became so angry with her, though. I stopped worrying about her hating me, or not loving me. I was too angry with them both. Every time they were pissed off with me, it just made it more obvious in my mind that they didn't understand me at all, and they never would.

'It's pathetic,' I said, under my breath, slamming the microwave door on a ready-meal I didn't even want.

I knew she'd heard me, but she pretended she hadn't.

'You can't have that for lunch, Emma, it's for-'

'Fine, Jesus, I don't even want it anyway. Would it be okay with you if I carried on breathing?'

'Don't start, Emma. Have a sandwich. There's lots-'

'I'm not hungry. Am I allowed to go to my room? Is that okay with you?'

She sighed and stood up.

'I'm taking Jake, now,' she said, 'why don't you help your dad with that flat-pack stuff. He's useless on his own.'

I didn't dignify it with a response. Instead, I decided to stay in my room all afternoon and make a point of not helping anyone with anything.

Lying on my bed, I looked up at the ceiling and thought about running away. *You can't*, I told myself. *You can't leave Jake. Besides, you need to be in Lulworth so you can see Anya.* I didn't acknowledge the other reason for staying - I couldn't leave them after what happened to Benji. But I didn't want to think about that. It was there, in the back of my mind, always. But I didn't like to bring it to the front.

I fell asleep and had a dream about being trapped in a microwave. Mum didn't know I was in there. I knew she was going to hit 'start' and it would kill me. I was screaming and banging on the glass, but I was the size of a penny and she couldn't hear me. The air was running out. I was gasping, trying to throw myself against the door to open it. She hit the button and I fell as the plate started to slowly rotate, taking me with it. I lay there, gasping, feeling my insides move in ways they shouldn't, like I was being torn apart. I couldn't move my limbs or turn my head, I was paralysed, looking at the white-hot lightbulb through the grill, getting hotter and hotter. It was blinding me, boiling my eyeballs. I could smell burning. Smoke.

I woke, shouting something. I struck my arm out involuntarily as I sat up, hitting the wall next to me, too hard. It broke the skin on my knuckle. I was panting, staring around the room. *You're awake*, I told myself. *You're awake. It was a dream.* I took a deep breath in through my nose, and out through my mouth. I could still smell burning. Smoke. I closed my eyes and shook my head, trying to rid it of the dream. But when I opened my eyes, the air looked hazy. It still smelled of smoke. *You're losing it*, I told myself. *Try again.* I did. It was still there when I opened them. I gripped my hands into the duvet and looked out of the window.

'Shit!'

Clouds of black-grey smoke were billowing up into the sky, reaching across from the fields over to our estate. It was coming from the facility. We lived close enough for me to see that there was a string of bedsheets tied together, flung from one of the windows, but there was nobody climbing down it. It barely reached halfway down the building. I jumped off the bed and ran downstairs.

'The Camp is on fire!' I shouted, 'we have to help, Dad, we have to-'

I ran into the living room to see mum and dad on the sofa, watching the news.

Rolling coverage of the fire.

'It's bad, isn't it?' Mum murmured, adding 'you alright, Emma? You've been asleep for ages. I've called Sam's mum. Jake's going to have to stay there tonight. Roads round here are all closed off.'

I watched the ticker along the bottom of the screen.

FIRE AT LULWORTH WORKER CAMP –
FIREFIGHTERS CALLED AFTER INCIDENT AT
FACILITY – FIRE BELIEVED TO HAVE STARTED
AT 2PM.

'It's been burning for hours,' I said, 'why is it still going? There's nobody left in there, is there?'

WORKERS TRAPPED INSIDE – FIRE
HAMPERING RESCUE EFFORTS

My knees buckled slightly. I held on to the sofa arm to steady myself. I felt vomit rise up and stumbled into the kitchen, retching over the sink. I lifted my head, watching the scene from the kitchen window. I could see the emergency services, crowded around the entrance. The entrance side was the one that faced our house. The yard was on the other side, behind. I prayed they were there, making their way out, out of the back door, across the yard. Firefighters were there, surely – with a ladder, over the railings. Or maybe they'd cut a section of them out. Created a passage. All the children would be there, standing on the field, watching, wrapped in foil blankets. Surely. About to be taken to safety.

I have to help.

I went into the hall and put my shoes on, then tried the door, as quietly as I could manage. *Locked*. My hands were shaking too much. I tried to calm my breathing.

'What are you doing?' Mum's voice hit me, like a dart in the back of my head.

'I have to help them,' I said, my voice faltering.

She put her hands over her face and rubbed her eyes, the same way she did when she grounded me.

'Keith,' she said, 'come here.'

Dad emerged.

'She's saying she wants to go there.'

'Well, I knew she would,' he said, looking at me, 'which is why all the doors and windows are locked, and you won't find the keys, no matter how hard you look.'

He smiled, then strolled back through to the TV.

'Just give up, Emma,' Mum said, quietly, 'there's nothing you can do. It's a horrible accident, and we just have to-'

I ran past her, to the back door, to try it. Then the kitchen windows, then through to the living room ones.

Tried them all.

'This is pointless, Emma,' Dad said, 'I'm not daft. You're wasting your time.'

I ran upstairs. *Come on. There must be one.* My room. Jake's room. Their room. The bathroom. I was crying. All I could see was Anya, banging on the windows, suffocating, gasping.

I ran back downstairs and kicked the door as hard as I could.

'Emma!' Dad shouted, charging through. I ran past him into the kitchen, looking for something heavy. The stone doorstop. It was a figure of a big, fat owl. I heaved it up, over my shoulder, aiming at the big window in the back door. He grabbed me.

'What *the fuck* do you think you're doing?!' he shouted, 'pack it in!'

We struggled. I dropped the owl and it crashed onto the floor, cracking the tiles.

'Fuck's sake, Emma!' Dad said, letting go of me. I crumbled, sobbing.

'Emma,' he started, softer, then stopped as I pushed past him. I ran up to my room and slammed the door, then stared out of the window.

It was worse. Darker, bigger, angrier. The flames were on every floor. I took a step closer, then another, slowly making my way to the bed, watching the clouds of smoke roll over and over. They kept coming. I knelt on the bed, gripping the windowsill. I felt tiny drops, my tears, splash on the back of my hands. I could barely blink. The blue lights of the emergency vehicles were flashing, but nothing was happening. I couldn't see anyone on the ground. *They're round the back*, I told myself. *They're getting them out, on the other side.*

Then I saw something moving. And another. Two figures, on the roof. They were adults. Men. They were waving their arms. I tried to see if anyone there could see them. Firefighters appeared, from the side of the building, scurrying to the truck, then back again. Some more started firing water into the flames. Huge jets, disappearing to nothing, swallowed by the smoke.

'Have they seen them?' I said out loud. I took out my phone. 999.

'What service do you require?'

'Fire. Ambulance. No, fire – it's the fire at Lulworth, there are two people on the roof and I don't think they've seen them-'

'We have lots of calls coming in about Lulworth. All our resources are there and I can assure you they're doing everything they can to evacuate the building and keep everyone nearby safe. I have to clear the line now. Goodbye.'

She hung up. I stared, listening to the dead tone, as one of the figures climbed over the edge of the roof. Just underneath, two windows flung open and flames belted out of them. He clung to the guttering. The other figure waved his arms, jumping up and down. Firefighters were still all over, some holding the jets of water steady, others disappearing into the building, then out again. Then I watched as the man clinging to the roof let go. I screamed, dropping my phone. The floor was hidden by the vehicles parked outside. As my eyes followed him down I caught sight of people, banging on the window. They must have seen him too.

I couldn't tell if they were men, women, children – but there were people there, two floors down, trying to get out. I saw an arm emerge; someone had punched through the glass. They knocked out the rest of it and clambered through, half in, half out of the window. It was too high to jump. They reached their arm towards a drainpipe, but at full-stretch they were still a foot short of it. I saw their arm fall back by their side. Then they swung both legs out and over, but something drew them back up and in, they were being pulled back inside by someone behind. I looked up and couldn't see the other man on the roof anymore. I searched across, but there was nothing on the roof except flames. My eyes darted back down, the person taken back inside was gone, replaced by a thick column of smoke.

'Stop watching, Emma,' my Mum said, 'come away.'

She came over and hugged me, pulling me away from the window. I couldn't speak. A voice in my head was screaming, but nothing would come out.

***

Good evening. You join me live from the studio for our news at ten on today, Saturday 17th April. Our top story: a fire breaks out at Lulworth Worker Camps, killing fifteen and injuring many more. The fire is believed to have been started following a riot, which broke out when a row between guards and Workers escalated. Several children are believed to be among the dead. Lulworth have not responded to reports that accommodation used to house the Workers was not compliant with fire safety regulations, or that overcrowding was to blame for a crush, which led to the suffocation of many.

I was curled up on my side, watching the scene live on TV, even though it was happening right behind me, outside the window.

All the windows and doors being closed didn't stop the smell. It wasn't a bonfire, autumn wood-burning scent. It was noxious, like if you burn something with paint on it or put plastic on a fire - it just sweats toxic fumes and makes you gag.

My body felt empty. I couldn't seem to do anything

except watch the same thing over and over. *Several children are believed to be among the dead. Children. Among the dead. Dead.*

I was useless. All I could do was hope Anya wasn't one of them.

I was grateful Jake wasn't with me. I would have snapped at him, shouted at him, made him cry, because he'd be asking me questions that I didn't want to answer.

Finally, I pushed my hands into the duvet and stretched away from it, lifting my weight. Sitting up felt cold and lonely. I was aware of the space around me, behind me. My head hurt so much. I hadn't eaten or drunk anything all day. I needed water. Painkillers. I took a deep breath and looked at the door. *Go downstairs, get them, come back, sleep. You have to turn the TV off.*

You need to eat. I thought about the chocolate digestives in the cereal cupboard, then felt guilty, because I'd earmarked them for Anya a few days earlier. I resolved to stay hungry until they let me out.

I walked out onto the landing, down the stairs, feeling like I wasn't really there. The living room door was open, so that the glare of the TV lit up the hall. The voice of the newsreader cut through. It was a different channel to the one I had on, so I stopped to listen, in case there was any new information.

The death toll has now risen from 15 to 18, including 11 children, according to the latest reports.

'Well,' I heard Dad's voice say, clearing his throat, 'plenty more where that came from.'

I stood for half a second, while the words sunk in. Then the blood seemed to rush round my system from nowhere, forcing me forwards, into the living room. I picked up the thick glass oblong vase off the sideboard and threw the flowers on the floor. The cat jumped off the chair and ran out into the hall, a black and white blur.

'Emma, what-' Mum started, then jerked backwards as I hurled the vase at the TV, watching the screen crack-smash and the whole thing sway backwards, then forwards, following the vase, crashing to the floor. They stared at the heap of glass shards and plastic, the big black shell of the TV leaning over it all. Then they stared at me.

'Don't worry,' I said, 'there's plenty more where that came from.'

***

Five weeks after the fire, once Lulworth had been cleared and closed, my parents finally let me out on my own.

'Can I come, Emmy?' Jake asked. 'Where are you going?'

I brushed his fringe out of his eyes and smiled. He looked confused.

'No, Jake, not today. I'll take you swimming tomorrow though, okay?'

He nodded, peeling the plastic label off the apple he was supposed to be eating.

'Still though, where are you going?' he persisted.

'To Lisa's.'

'Oh,' he said, wrinkling his nose. I knew it would put him off. He hated Lisa, ever since she told on him for trying to give her Persian cat a haircut.

Breathing the air outside, walking alone, nobody watching or waiting - it felt so good. I could go anywhere. I thought about it. I even sat at the bus stop for a bit, watching them come and go. I almost got on one to the train station.

I couldn't decide what to do. The sky was grey,

rolling. I decided, before anything else, I had to say goodbye.

I went the back way. The front route to Lulworth was blocked off with construction vehicles, shipping containers, Worker Transits. They were turning the site into a shopping centre. The whole thing had been stripped down to the foundations, but they hadn't taken the railings around the perimeter down. I hiked up the scrubland slope that led to the spot we used to meet Anya, right at the furthest point away from the building, on the edge of the boundary.

I could see her there, gripping the railings, waiting for me to pull the tooth. I could see the spot where she lay, blood seeping from the corner of her mouth, the patch where she spat the infection out, the grass her tooth lay in.

'I hope you're alive,' I said, to the space she used to stand in. Tears were in my eyes. I was angry with myself for crying. At first I tried not to let them fall, soaking them with my sleeve before they had chance. Then I saw something, a package, just on my side of the railings, under the shaggy fringes of the long grass.

I stepped forwards then knelt down, sweeping the grass to one side with my wet sleeve. A cloud of tiny flies burst upwards from something next to it, dog poo maybe, I thought. *No.* I winced and dragged the paper bundle in the other direction with my fingertips. It was something wrapped in newspaper.

I sat back on the grass and peeled away the paper. It was damp and disintegrating, coming to pieces in my hands. I opened out the last fold and as soon as I saw it, dropped the whole thing like a match had burned down to my finger. A scrap of newspaper torn from a blank edge had tiny pencil writing on it.

Emmy and Jake
You didn't come when we said, so I left these here in case you come
later. Jake, the fruit is for you. Emmy, I told you I'd bring you
something! Sorry, there's nothing else I could use here!
Lots of love,
Anya xxx

I gave up trying to stop the tears. I sobbed, looking over
at the grass pile where the flies had been. I reached over
and swept the grass aside again. The flies clouded up then
settled back down. It smelt rotten-sweet, like when dad
tried to make cider in the shed. There was the alien fruit -
what was left of it. The stones were still there, submerged
in glossy goop, orange-purple red, speckled and rippling
with flies. I buried my face in the inside of my elbow to
soak some of the tears, and the snot, but it kept coming.
I looked back at the paper and took a deep breath.

My fingers were shaking because I'd already seen
what was in there. Unfolding the paper, there it was
again, her gleaming white tooth. Tied up in red cotton
strands, plaited and secured around it in a cross, two
sides reaching out and branching round in a near circle.

It was a bracelet, made from the cotton from her
cardigan, the one she used to clean the blood from her
tooth that day. One end split into two plaits, then back
into one, to make a small buttonhole. On the other side a
white button was threaded onto the end, closing finally
with all the loose ends knotted together. I fastened it
round my wrist and put the note in my pocket.

After one last look at the alien-fruit remains, I set off
down the hill, holding my fingers over the tooth-jewel,
taking my new pulse.

***

That day, I vowed to search for Anya, forever, if that's how long it took. This is the story of how I found her.

Chapter 4

Dear Parents/Carers,
The final payment for the Berlin trip is now due.

I inhaled and walked into the kitchen. *They don't suspect anything. Calm down. Just get the money.*

'I have to give them the final payment, if that's okay?' I said, handing the note to Mum. She took it without looking up, scrolling down her timeline on her phone. I watched her fingernails. Always so neat. Mine were ragged, bitten, ugly. She always had smoothly filed ovals and just one coat of clear varnish, showing the tip of a half-moon at the bottom of her perfectly pushed back cuticles.

'It says you need a decent warm coat,' she murmured, finally scanning the letter. 'We can't afford a new one on top of this so you'll just have to borrow my green one. For god's sake, don't lose this one, yeah?'

'I won't.'

She looked at me.

'Who else is going on this trip?'

'Most of the group.'

'Don't drink. Or smoke anything weird. You're really vulnerable as a young girl over there, it's full of-'

'I'll be fine, Mum. It's a school trip.'

'They're the worst! I remember when we went to London with my school - Christ. How we came back alive I don't know. They just let us run riot. It's different abroad, though, especially in a country like that.'

I didn't rise to it. We had to be on good terms, otherwise the whole thing could be off. I couldn't afford any more arguments. I needed to behave well enough for them to let me go to Berlin with school, but not behave *so well* that they'd suspect I was up to something. A rescue mission. An escape.

I took the cash up to my room and thanked god she didn't trust online banking anymore. The girl who sat next to me in History was going on the trip. I saw her receipts for her payments, they were easy to forge - just two lines of Times New Roman with a gap for the pupil's name and the payment amount to be handwritten. I printed them off while my parents were at work and prayed they didn't speak to school before the trip left. There was no danger of that, though. They were too busy. Dad was doing night shifts on the new plant, mum was doing extra hours to pay medical bills. She was preoccupied with Jake. He had some symptoms that were like Benji's. The headaches, trouble sleeping. Everyone was still getting used to paying for healthcare. Non-emergency healthcare, that is. Investigations weren't an emergency. Even if you might have the same thing your brother died of.

'Emmy?'

'Jake,' I said, stuffing the money under my pillow, 'you need to learn to knock.'

'Sorry.'

He dawdled in the doorway. I looked at him. Whatever it was, he was struggling to say it.

'What is it, Jake?'

'When you go to Berlin, can I come?'

'No, you can't. It's just for the people in my class.'

He looked at the floor, clinging to the door frame with one hand and rubbing the back of his head with the other.

'What's up?' I asked.

'My head hurts. How long will you be away for?'

'Just a few days.'

I felt like shit. The worst sister. A terrible human being. I knew he would sense something was wrong before anyone else did, before everyone started to panic. He could always tell when I was up to something. I still regret what it did to him. You don't understand how much you can hurt the people who love you when you're young, though. Or at least, I didn't, anyway.

'I don't want you to go,' he said, finally looking up at me.

No. Don't do this to me.

'Don't worry about me, Jake, I'll be fine.'

'I'm not worried about *you*, I'm worried about *me*. I'll be lonely.'

'Come here,' I said, patting the bed next to me. He came over and sat heavily by my side, so I grabbed him in a bear hug like I used to when he was smaller. It also meant he couldn't see the tears in my eyes. I blinked them away.

You can't do this to him, a voice in my head said. *But what about Anya? She has no-one. Jake will be fine. He has Mum and Dad. She could be trafficked. Sold into slavery. Killed. You have to try to help her.*

He'll forgive you. One day.

***

'Right. Are you sure you've packed everything? I still think it's daft that they're making you camp out.'

'Only on one of the nights. It's the project they've got going on with the homeless refug-'

'-don't,' she interrupted me, 'you've said already. Makes me feel sick. With worry, I mean. It doesn't sound safe at all. I asked Laura's mum what she thought.'

Shit. Shit. When did she see her?

'She said she didn't even know it was happening,' Mum carried on, 'but she thought it was a good idea. Teach you all *empathy.*' She rummaged through the front pocket of my rucksack to check its contents. 'That's Ruth for you though, total airhead. Doesn't have a clue. No idea about the real world. Still, she said Danny did something similar last year on their Paris trip and apparently you don't actually stay in the same place as them. It's just a mock-up, to show you what it's like.'

Thank god. By the time all this unravels, I'll have a decent head-start at least.

That night, I couldn't sleep. I glanced over at my phone. The screen glowed with a notification to indicate it was finally charged. I turned over and stared at the ceiling. I had no idea what I'd be looking at tomorrow night. The roof of a bus station? A doorway? The sky?

Why are you doing this?

I shook the question from my mind and went through the list of items in my head. *Money. Sleeping bag. Torch. Underwear. Warm coat. Toothbrush. Toothpaste. Gloves. Walking boots.* I turned over again and tossed the duvet down to the bottom of the bed. It was too hot. My hair was starting to stick to my neck. I sat up, pulled it all up into a bun and fumbled in the half-light for a hairband on the bedside table. My fingers felt the photo frame and stopped. I exhaled, letting my hair fall back down. I picked up the picture and held it next to my chest, closing my eyes. It was the photo of Benji and Jake that mum gave me after Benji's funeral.

You have to come back alive, I said to myself. *They can't go through it again.*

I went over the plan in my mind again and tried to remember what the journalist said, the day I walked into the Herald's office and asked to see the reporter who covered the Lulworth story.

'She's busy. I can take a message,' the man on reception said.

'Is she here?'

'I can take a message,' he repeated, 'but she's busy right now.'

'I can wait.'

He rolled his eyes and sighed, locking his computer screen. He pushed himself back from the desk and got up, then shot me a look as he backed through the door behind him into the large, open plan office.

I stood on my tiptoes and leaned forward to see if I could spot her through the small pane of glass in the door. His face appeared again and startled me. I took a step back as he opened the door.

'She'll be five minutes,' he said, sitting back down. 'Don't touch any of the artwork.'

I hadn't realised I had my hand on a sculpture that was reaching up from the coffee table. I retracted my fingers and looked at it. It was a hand, a child's arm and hand outstretched, made from stone, maybe. It made me feel weird. Cold. The caption on the plinth said: *Lost at Sea*. I felt sick.

'Hello? Are you Emma?' a voice said, snapping me back from a place I didn't want to be.

'Yes,' I said, smiling, grateful. 'I just wanted to ask you about the Lulworth story. I had a friend who was in the fire, you see, and I wondered if you-'

'-come on,' she interrupted me, walking towards the entrance, 'I'm due a break anyway, let's get some fresh air.'

I followed her.

'How old are you?' she asked, as we sat down with our drinks.

'Sixteen,' I lied.

'Hm. How old was your friend?'

'Fourteen. She had her birthday there.'

'What do you know about the fire?'

She eyed me, stirring the foam around her coffee. I hesitated.

'Well, nothing, really, just what's been on the news-'

'-keep your voice down,' she said, glancing around the room.

I shut up.

'I don't have the proof I need yet,' she said in a hushed voice, 'but they have blood on their hands. No question. All this bullshit about a riot, don't believe it.'

'But why would they-'

'-to show what happens when you protest,' she said, 'you die. Your family dies. Nobody cares.'

'No,' I shook my head, 'stuff like that doesn't happen in this country. Not even to Workers. I mean, things are bad, but they wouldn't *kill* people…'

'No,' she pointed her finger at me, with a half-smile, 'but they'd *let them die*. Didn't you see the emergency services just sitting like lemons outside the gates?'

'They weren't just sat outside – I saw them coming in and out of the building, they had the hoses and – I mean, they couldn't get the people off the roof or from the top floors, but that's because it was too dangerous-'

'Bollocks was it.' She sipped her coffee and shook her head. 'Anyway,' she said, placing her cup back on its saucer, 'what did you want to know?'

'I'm trying to find my friend. I don't know if she died, or if she was evacuated. If she's alive, I want to know where she was taken. You hear things...I just want to know if she's okay.'

She smiled, apologetically. Her eyes told me I had no chance. She took a deep breath.

'Chances are, if she didn't die, she was evacuated with the rest and taken to Calais.'

'Calais? Why?'

'Everyone at Lulworth was classed as High Risk after the fire. Even the kids.'

'What does that mean?'

'No good for work in the UK, but they might put them to work abroad somewhere. Somewhere rules don't interfere with things. Calais is where they sort them out.'

That's when I decided to run away.

***

'Honestly, you don't need to drop me off. I'm fine. I can get the bus.'

'Your rucksack weighs more than *you* do, Emma,' Mum said, 'let your Dad give you a lift for gods' sake.'

'Can I come?' asked Jake, 'and watch you get on the coach?'

Shit. My mind went blank. Everything was about to crash down; I could feel it.

'You don't have time, Jake,' Mum said, 'we're going to school now. Say bye-bye.'

I exhaled. Jake pouted.

'Come here,' I said, stretching out my arms, 'I want your best hug, please.'

He half-smiled and stepped towards me, a proper smile breaking out across his face when repeated *best hug*. I grabbed him and held him tight, breathing in his smell. *Oh god. Keep it together*, I told myself, trying to swallow down the lump in my throat.

'Keith!' Mum shouted upstairs, 'Emma needs to be there for half past, yeah?' she waited, listening, then rolled her eyes. 'He's in the shower. Don't let him get you late.'

She grabbed her keys off the side and bustled Jake towards the door.

'Oh,' she said, turning around, 'bye, sweetheart.'

She hesitated for a second, then stumbled back through into the kitchen under the weight of her bags. She reached out and held the back of my head, then strained across to kiss my forehead.

'Be good.'

I watched them go and started to feel nauseous.

I heard the shower screen swing open upstairs. My heart was beating so hard I could see the fabric of my top tick where it stretched over my chest. *Come on, do it.*

'Dad?' I called up.

'Yeah?'

'I'm off now.'

'Hang on, I can give you a lift.'

'No, don't worry, Misha called me, her mum can pick me up from the main road.'

I held my breath.

'Alright,' he shouted down, 'see you Thursday then. Just text me when you pass the services. Have a good trip.'

I exhaled and grabbed my bag. *Christ, that's heavy.*

'Will do, see you,' I shouted back, hauling the rucksack above my shoulders and grappling my arms through. 'Bye!'

***

The coach to Dover took £40 out of my envelope of cash and ten hours out of my life. It makes me laugh, now, that I felt so hard done to. Ten hours on a coach with seats, windows, air conditioning and a toilet. I could, eat, drink. Get up, walk around. I had the ability to get off, if I really wanted to. To know where I was going, to know when I'd get there. To talk to the driver, other passengers, without risking my life. To know the date, the time, whether it was dark or light outside. I could have even called someone to come and get me if I'd wanted to. I spent half the time browsing the news on my phone, for god's sake.

Soon enough, I would look back on that coach journey as the height of luxury. Fantasise about the scratchy nylon seat covers, the smudged windows, the toilet seat dappled with dark urine. But at the time, sat watching the endless grey track outside, dozing, then waking with terror at the realisation of what I'd done - I thought I might lose my mind.

When we finally got to Dover, I knew I had to throw my phone away. I should've done it back home, really, but I knew CCTV could track me to Dover anyway. I might as well be able to do some planning before I gave it up. I took out my notebook and copied down the emergency numbers. Mum. Dad. Misha. I made a mental note to keep trying to memorise them in case I lost my bag.

I scrolled through the timelines. The ones that made me feel as though I was doing the right thing. *We're All Workers, Resist4Good, AllofUs.* The videos I watched again and again, the accounts from in the camps and the testimonies from the holding facilities. One with a young girl, like me, who had joined AllofUs and was volunteering in a camp in Hungary. I couldn't place her accent, Eastern European maybe. She couldn't have been much older than me. She was talking to an interviewer who was off camera, explaining her choices.

'Why did you come here?' he asked.

'Because I couldn't just stay at home and do nothing. People are dying. They're being persecuted, raped, tortured, starved, drowned. If this happened where you lived, wouldn't you want someone to help you? Just because it doesn't happen now, doesn't mean it won't soon. We are one world. We can't just turn away.'

No. I won't turn away.

Another video showed Workers who had been deported as 'High Risk', like Anya. They were being led into a courtyard. The camera was shaky, behind a chain-link fence. You could see the men in boots and peaked caps with their guns slung low, occasionally shoving one of the Workers back into line. They barked orders and the line began to separate. Children on one side, adults on the other. Suddenly one of the guards turns and sees they're being filmed. He shouts, marching towards the fence, hand on his gun. The film stops.

Anya could be there.

Then, the picture that sealed everything for me. The picture that made me feel like I was standing on the edge of a cliff, watching people fall onto the rocks. They were never next to me on the cliff top. They just appeared, one foot away from me, off the edge in the air, like a flickering image appearing on a screen, suddenly there, terrified, then pushed off balance, they would fall and I would watch their disappearing hands grappling, their eyes scream. The picture was of a body, washed up on the shore. It was tiny. A child's body. A toddler. The photo went everywhere. You will have seen it. On all the front pages. The photo that finally made people care, for a few days at least. He was perfect, just like Benji. You couldn't see his face because it was buried in the sand. But the little curls of his hair, the chubby forearms and calves, his t-shirt and shorts, the grey-white socks and blue shoes with their Velcro fastenings. His tiny fingers, gripping the sand.

The photo was often posted in context, in its use as the front page of The Sentry, including the first line of the story: *Three years after the Workers initiative was brought in, migrants are still drowning.*

Then the caption from the post: *If you're not part of the solution, you're part of the problem.*

I will be part of the solution, I told myself. *I will do something.*

I turned my phone off and looked up. The air was just starting to get cold. I'd been hanging around at the entrance of the car park for twenty minutes, it was time to throw the phone away. I walked up to the bin, glanced around and threw it in. It was full. *There's a chance it could be emptied tomorrow, then. Might give me some time.*

The lorry I'd been eyeing up sat there, dirty white and massive, like someone had hauled an aisle from a grotty supermarket and dropped it in the middle of Dover.

Alright. Let's do this.

I looked around. There was no security, as far as I could tell. After all, everyone wanted to get in, but who wanted to *leave* illegally? Nobody in their right mind. I had to. I had my passport, just in case, but if I could get out without a trace, it would buy me some time. I walked as though I was about to get into one of the cars parked next to the lorry, then fumbled in my pocket as though I was trying to find my keys. I got to the boot of the Corsa parked next to it and looked around again. A man a few cars down was rummaging in his boot. I yawned, pretending to fix the zip on my hoodie. He closed the boot and walked off. The edge of the lorry was right next to me. I wondered what was inside and prayed it wasn't refrigerated. I put my hand on the steel rod that ran down the back edge and took a deep breath. I ran my fingers along the length of it, down to the bottom and across to the middle where it met the hinge of the door. There was a handle just within reach. *It's not going to be open.* I looked at the lock and tried the door. Locked. *Fuck.*

A noise made me drop to the floor, instinctively. The concrete was wet. I scrambled backwards to the shadows behind the Corsa, grazing the edge of my hand. I saw his feet, through the gap between the car and the floor. They scuffed along the concrete, tiny droplets sparking out from under his soles. He stopped at the back of the lorry, by the door I'd just tried. *Shit.*

Pins and needles started to creep through my legs, lactic acid seizing up the joints. My knees and hands were in the puddle next to the car. I could feel the gritty silt in the cold water getting under my fingernails and through my jeans. My neck ached with the effort of keeping my head up off the floor, craning sideways to see underneath. The rucksack seemed to weigh ten times more than me, straining over to one side, threatening to topple me over. *What is he doing?*

I heard metal, clinking. He was opening the door. I heard a thud. Dropping something in, maybe. Then a slam. His feet shuffled back over to the front and opened the driver side door. *He didn't lock the back. Now. Now or never.*

I waited to hear the driver's door slam shut and got to my feet, still crouching low. The blood returned to my legs and my feet stung with the prickles of each step. I stepped around the back of the car and looked at his wing-mirror. His face was lit up with the blue-white light of his phone. Middle-aged. Shaved head. I ran across to the door, my rucksack jolting me from side to side, then held the handle and tried to open it as slowly and quietly as possible.

The door swung open, faster than I expected, nearly knocking me to the ground. My feet faltered before I grabbed the edge of the closed door and hauled myself up, reaching for the other to bring it closed behind me.

Fuck. How could I close it without making a noise? It was designed to be shut from the outside. I had to pull it with some real force. It would slam. He would hear and come find me. I couldn't leave it open though.

The engine started and the radio sparked up, blaring out metal music. It was so loud. *Go on.* I hauled the door and let go. It slammed. All the blood drained from my limbs and I found myself running to the back of the container in the dark, clambering over something, crouching behind something else. Boxes, crates, maybe. I waited to hear the slam of his door and the footsteps round the back. I was panting. I could smell damp cardboard and something else. Something earthy, sour. The straps of my rucksack dug into my shoulders and my back was wet with sweat under the weight. Again, I nearly fell over. Backwards this time. The music continued. The engine carried on. Still, no door, no footsteps. Suddenly the whole thing lurched forwards and I fell back. Scrambling to my feet, I realised the whole thing was on the move - and I was going with it.

Chapter 5

I woke with a jolt. This was a talent I would soon perfect
- the ability to fall asleep anywhere, however
uncomfortable, whatever the imminent danger. I didn't
do well on that first journey. Fifteen minutes, maybe.
For what felt like the first half hour, the engine and the
radio drowned everything out. We were stop-start,
constantly. Barriers, border checks, boarding, I hoped.
Each time the motion slowed to a halt, I was convinced
that light would flood in and an angry voice would bark
at me. It never did, though.

The noises changed. We weren't outside anymore, I
could tell. We were still moving, but it wasn't the lorry. It
felt like we'd driven into a warehouse, parked up, then
the whole thing had cut adrift and set off down the road.

I prayed we were sailing.

I kept trying to listen, to feel. There was only white
noise and a gentle lull. I stared for what seemed like
forever in the slow rumbling dark, sat in a corner,
between boxes, hugging my knees. Then, somewhere
along the way, I closed my eyes.

When I woke my neck was stiff. Still the slow
rumble carried on in the background. It was warm now,
stifling, even. I turned my head from side to side and
touched my chin to my chest. The ache was worst across
my shoulders. I still hadn't dared to take my rucksack off.

I wished I had my phone. I had a watch but couldn't see the time in the dark. I'd never worn a watch in my life. My phone was usually my watch. My grandmother left me a Marcasite in her will and it had sat in a box on my bookshelf ever since. Finally, it was feeling a pulse again. So incongruous - silver, sparkly, slender next to my fraying hoodie sleeve and bitten fingernails. My other wrist had Anya's bracelet on. I had bandaged over the tooth with a red ribbon, to avoid questions from mum. I told her it was a friendship bracelet from Misha. I squinted at the watch face. *Get the torch out*, I told myself, *at least you can see the time then.*

I struggled to free my arms from inside the rucksack straps and leaned forward. The blessed relief of stretching forwards made me forget myself and I let out a sound, a kind of sigh, a moan. I caught myself and retracted my arms, staring round in the dark, listening.

The gentle jostle continued. I got to my knees and swivelled round, overbalancing to my left side. My elbow clattered into something that moved, my ribs into something that didn't. *Shit*. I stopped and listened.

Nothing.

The torch was right at the bottom of the bag. I finally retrieved it and sat back against the rucksack, clicking the switch up. I held my hand over the torch face at first, blinking at the light glowing between my fingers. I turned the torch upside down so that the light was against my stomach. Bending my wrist towards the light, I let it move a fraction away from my body so the watch was illuminated. The ornate hands pointed to 2:45. *Nearly 3am.* I turned the torch round to the thing I'd fallen into earlier. It was a stack of crates, wooden ones on the bottom, cardboard on top. Mushrooms. That was the smell. Beyond that, the light was dim. More boxes, crates, a canister of gas, something with wheels and a lever.

The noises changed. Doors. Things around us were moving. I clicked the torch light off and held my breath. The engine started up again. The music thrashed out for a few seconds before it stopped. I put my arms back inside the straps of my rucksack and gripped them, resisting the urge to scratch my nose. Something was crawling on it. When it fell off, I realised it was a bead of sweat. I rubbed my sleeve over my face. We jolted backwards, then started slowly moving forwards. *Shit. This is it.*

We finally made our way outside. I could tell from the air. Still full of fumes, but cold. I breathed in deep, as though breathing it would cool me down. The light was different, too. When we were inside, there was nothing. Now we were outside, a small crease all the way around the doors betrayed the streetlights, just a glimmer of electric in the black.

I suddenly realised I had no idea what to do. *When do I get out? How?* I ran through all the different scenarios and realised there was almost no chance of doing it without meeting the driver. The door only opened from the outside. He had to open it for me to get out. Unless he left it open and unguarded - which would never happen in Calais - I would have to meet him. Then a worse thought crossed my mind. *What if he doesn't open it at all?* I started to breathe too fast. I couldn't control it. Like when you cry as a kid and you gasp for breath over and over and you can't get your rhythm back. *Calm down,* I heard my mum say, *breathe in through your nose and out through your mouth, slowly.* I tried it. My head swam.

Mushrooms. This stuff is perishable. It won't last long. He has to open the doors soon.

I realised I was crying. *Don't. Don't listen.* The voice that told me I was stupid, I'd put myself in danger, I was going to destroy my family, was getting louder and louder.

'Shut up!' I found myself shouting.

I stopped. We weren't moving any more. No music. The engine was off. Footsteps, round the side of the van. *He heard me.* My mind was blank. I had no story. No excuse. Nothing. I remember the sharp scratch of metal in metal, the key turning, watching the light glimmer as the door rattled, then shrinking behind the crate when the light flooded in. Why did I bother? He would find me.

'Hello?' he called.

I was shaking. *What's the worst he can do? He can call the police. Call mum.* I thought of the piece of paper with all my numbers on.

'Oi!' he shouted, 'I've had enough of you scumbags thinking you can get one over on me. Come out here so I can kick your fucking head in!'

I jumped up, nearly falling over under the weight of my rucksack as I stumbled forwards, hands in the air.

'I'm sorry, I'm sorry!' I cried. I kept repeating it. I didn't know what else to say.

'What *the fuck* are you doing in my lorry?' he demanded. His face was so angry. His voice was even angrier. I don't know what I was expecting - shock, confusion, maybe, but not rage.

'I didn't mean any harm,' I faltered, 'I - I was drunk and I fell asleep and-'

He hauled himself into the trailer and lunged towards me. He was about a foot taller than me, well built. His hand gripped around my arm. I couldn't see his face anymore. The light was behind him.

'You think you can just catch a free ride? Get me arrested?' His breath smelled like his gums were rotting. I winced, shaking my head. He squeezed my arm tighter. 'I've had girls like you in here before, you know. Other way, of course. They want to get into the UK. They'll do anything, *anything* to ride in this fucking lorry.'

He shoved me and I toppled instantly, dragged backwards by my rucksack. I tried to haul myself up but he was on top of me, pinning my shoulders. All I could see was a triangle of light between his left shoulder and ear. Everything inside the outline of his ear, neck, collarbone, was black. The smell of his breath, the heat, the damp mushrooms, sweating in the dark, all closed in on me. I was drowning. I couldn't feel my legs. I couldn't breathe. Was he kneeling on me?

'I don't care who you are,' he said, 'you pay. They all pay.'

He moved one hand and reached down. I couldn't push him off. I could barely lift my head. My arm was free, though. I grabbed the first thing I felt. Crate. No good. I reached further. Metal. The window of light behind him got smaller as he leaned closer. He grabbed at my jeans. The window disappeared.

***

I was staring out at the road, panting. We were parked up on a grass verge, off a main road. Dawn was breaking. Every now and then a car or a truck would cut through the gloaming, lights still on. They couldn't see us. I turned to look at him. I'd been there for 30 seconds, maybe a minute, but it felt like hours. Just staring out of the end of the trailer, my mind blank.

What are you doing? Get out of here.

He still might die. You might have killed him. I couldn't give the thought room; it made my limbs too weak to move. I couldn't remember exactly what had happened, how I did it, but I knew I'd hit him. The gas canister lay on the floor, blood on one side. I don't remember him falling. Maybe I pushed him off. I remember being terrified that he was dead, then seeing his chest rise and fall. I should have run when I saw him breathing. Instead I just stopped, unable to process what had just happened, or what to do next, staring out of the doors. *Come on.* I stepped over his body and picked up my rucksack. I needed to be sick.

I looked down at him, trying not to vomit. *He's still breathing.* His leg started to shift. I ran.

***

Before the Assessment Camps were closed down, there were a few in Calais. A lot of the charities based themselves there. I suppose if Step 1 of my plan was to get to Calais, this was Step 2.

I must have looked horrendous. A man opened the gate in the chain-link fence and spoke French. I could vaguely follow. I got an award for French in Year 8, so I'd chosen it for GSCE. I tried to answer him as best I could. The gist was, he wanted to know if I was okay and where I'd come from. I told him: *I'm okay. I've come from England to volunteer.* He looked confused. No wonder. It was about 5 or 6 in the morning. I stood in front of him, 5ft 3, clinging to the straps of a rucksack that reached the back of my knees at one end and above my head on the other, hair wet with cold sweat.

I mumbled something about a difficult journey and an email that had gone missing. Or that's what I hoped I'd said, anyway. He asked me who I was volunteering with. *Shit. He believes me. For now, anyway. AllofUs,* I said, because I could say it in French too. He nodded, motioning for me to come in.

'Where's your phone?' he said, in English. 'I'll show you the app, it helps with translation.'

'It was stolen,' I said, 'on the way here.'

'Are you okay? Did you speak to the police?'

'I'm fine… no, I didn't. They didn't hurt me. I didn't see their face,' I said, thinking of the lorry driver's silhouette.

'You should report it. Come on, I'll take you to the place. They won't be up yet, but I can show you somewhere to rest.'

There were a few tents, huddled together at one end of the camp, for the charity workers. They looked smaller, tattier than the ones we'd passed for the government workers. *Still,* I thought, *better than whatever the Workers are in.*

I waited until he'd gone, to cry. Relief. Fear. I sobbed into my sleeve, sat on the camp-bed. I tried to be quiet. Three other people were asleep in the same tent. I tried not to think about Jake. *Would they even know I was missing yet? Probably not.* I hoped not. School didn't know I was missing from home. They never thought I was going on the trip. As far as they were concerned, I was on summer break, with my parents. My parents thought I was with school, in Berlin. Surely that bought me a few days.

Mum will worry when you don't message her to tell her you've arrived. She'll ask Misha's mum if she's heard from her. Or maybe not. She's doing extra shifts this week. Might take longer.

I wiped my face with my sleeve and looked at the bed. I knew I needed sleep, but it seemed impossible. There was an older woman in the bunk next to me. She had ginger dreadlocks and tattoos on her neck. She was snoring. Across the way, there was a boy. *Probably older than me*, I thought, *but only just.* I sniffed the last of the tears away and stared at him. He was beautiful. Dark hair, eyelashes and eyebrows. A hint of a moustache. I smiled. It looked like my mum's did when she was late bleaching it. I placed a bet with myself. *His eyes are green. Hazel. Brown. No, green. What are you doing? Get some sleep.*

I lay down on the thin mattress above the creaking springs, wincing at the noise. The tattooed lady shifted. Her face was opposite mine. Uncomfortably close, for a stranger. I could feel her breath, just the very end of it, as it dispersed. Just the faintest wave of heat, moisture in the air. A smell like damp earth. I closed my eyes. The smell of the lorry driver lingered. He was on my clothes, in my hair, coating the space between my mouth and my nose. I wanted to leave my body there, on the bed, and be somewhere else.

It's too late for that.

***

Singing. Someone was singing. For the shortest time, I thought I was at home. Before I opened my eyes, when I was still shifting in the early mist of waking, I thought I could see my bedside table, the photo of Benji and Jake, my dressing gown on the back of the door. Then, I had a moment of blind panic when I didn't know where I was. I turned over, looked up and remembered where I was, and why. The woman with the dreadlocks was singing something I didn't recognise, but I liked. She saw I was awake.

'Toma says you're a new volunteer,' she said, smiling, 'but you had a rough journey. Are you okay?'

I sat up and pulled my hoodie on. I hadn't noticed the cold when I got there, but there was no escaping it now. It had settled into my bones while I slept. It was too cold for the time of year. I didn't dare think what it must be like in winter.

'I'm fine,' I lied.

'I'm Julia,' she said, holding her hand out.

I shook it. Her skin was rough.

'I'm E- Ellie' I stuttered, realising as I was about to say *Emma* that I couldn't use my real name.

'What are you doing here, Dima?' A gruff voice barked. The fourth person in the tent was up. I hadn't realised there was a man in the tent with us. He'd had his sleeping bag over his head all night. He was older than my dad. Weather-beaten. Grey-brown tufts of hair curled around the edges of his woollen hat. His beard reminded me of a hedgehog - white and brown spines that seemed to bristle all on their own. He stood over the boy, who was still asleep.

'Dima!' he shouted, shoving the boy's shoulder.

He woke with a start.

Green. I knew it.

'What?' Dima asked, blinking.

'How did you get in here? These aren't your quarters. You know that. Just because you can sweet-talk Julia, don't think you can get around me too. There are rules for a reason. You have to follow them in a place like this, or everything breaks down, yeah?'

Dima smiled, stretching.

'I'm sorry Gerald. From the bottom of my heart,' he said, patting his chest with his hand.

'Hmm,' said Gerald, turning around and picking up a kettle from the floor, 'less of your cheek, please.'

'What is *cheek*?' Dima asked.

'Ignore Gerald,' Julia said, 'he's always grumpy in the morning.'

Dima looked at me.

'Hello,' he said, waving, as though we were miles apart.

'Hi,' I replied, with a quick show of my palm. My shy wave.

'This is Ellie,' said Julia to Dima and Gerald. 'She's a

new volunteer. Got lost and robbed on her way here though. Had a bit of a shit time, so be nice to her.'
Dima smiled. I couldn't tell if it was a genuine smile, or a smirk.

Gerald lit the calor-gas stove and placed the kettle over it.

'Tea?' he asked. 'You look cold. It's summer, but it's a really cold one. This weather's set in for a couple of weeks at least. Have you got everything they told you to bring? The list?'

'I didn't get one...I had to guess.'

'Hmm. Need warm clothes. Waterproof ones, too.'

'I can find you some,' interrupted Dima.

'Dima is just leaving,' said Gerald. 'He's supposed to be in the refugee quarters. *Not* the charity ones. But he's a cheeky bugger.'

'Is *cheeky* like *cheek*?' Dima asked.

'You know it is. Don't pretend your English isn't good. Go on. Away with you.'

Dima got up. 'I'm going, I'm going.' He pulled on his coat and hat. 'Nice to meet you, Ellie.'

I smiled, watching him leave.

***

'Do you think I could find someone if they were here?' I asked Julia.

'How do you mean?' she asked, wringing out washing over the basin.

'I'm looking for a friend.'

She could be so close. She might just be down in the camp. I wondered if her family were with her, or if she was alone.

'You're looking for someone?' Julia said, frowning, looking at me sideways while she hung the wet clothes on the rack.

'Yeah. Not - I mean, I'm here as a volunteer, obviously, but it's just… I had a friend…who was in a Worker Camp. Did you hear about the Lulworth fire?'

Julia nodded.

'She was in it. And I don't know what happened to her. I thought she might be here.'

Julia shook her head. 'I doubt it, she'll probably be in another Worker Camp, don't you think? This is a camp for refugees.'

'All Workers started out as refugees though, didn't they? None of them went to other Worker Camps after the fire. They - well, the survivors - were labelled High Risk. They all come here, right?'

'Some of them do, yeah. Not all.'

Shit.

She sat on the bunk opposite me, looking serious. 'How old are you?'

'Sixteen,' I lied.

'I told them we shouldn't take anyone under eighteen. Doesn't seem right. You came here to volunteer, though, didn't you? Not just to see if your friend is here?'

'No, no of course,' I stammered, 'I-'

'Because this is intense, Ellie. It's not for the faint-hearted. People's lives are at stake, here. We're all they have. The only thing that stands between them and the abyss. Sometimes we can't save them. Sometimes we can. Sometimes all we can do is make the journey less horrific. It's not a game, Ellie. It's people's lives.'

Her voice was stern. The way she was looking at me made me uncomfortable.

'I know,' I said, quietly, 'I know. I'm here to help. *AllofUs,*' I said, as though repeating a mantra. 'I joined to come here and make a difference. I just… I thought, if she were here, I could help her, too.'

Julia's face softened. She nodded.

'Of course. I see that. We can't search the database, that's the government's. You could ask them, but they're not exactly forthcoming. Chances are, though, you'll meet her, if she's here. There are hundreds of people, but we're all living on top of each other. Ask around.'

'I will,' I said, nodding. 'Thank you.'

I'd better get started, I thought.

It was worse than the videos. Gerald said it was best for me to *get stuck in straight away* and he'd get me started in the medical tent. I was desperate for a wee, so I asked him where the toilets were as we walked.

'Oh, well, there's one portaloo for the charity workers back at the tents. Do you want to go back?'

I turned and looked back. It was raining and we were at the bottom of a hill.

'No, it's alright, I'll use the ones in the camp.'

'Hmm. Good luck.'

If you've ever walked past a bin lorry on a hot day, you'll know the smell that was getting stronger with each step we took towards the main camp. The noise got louder and louder, too. A murmur of voices, shouting, singing, arguing, laughing. Children playing. The sounds of clanking metal, paper crumpling, plastic sheeting blowing in the wind. We finally reached the point where the sea of worn beige tents met the muddy verge, separated by more chain-link fence. A guard opened the gate, eyeing me.

'She's new,' said Gerald, 'not got her badge yet.'

I still wasn't used to seeing guns. The police in the UK hardly ever used them then. Every now and then you'd see some armed police, walking around crowded places like a shopping mall, but it was rare. I never knew if it was in response to a genuine threat, or just to reassure people. Either way, I didn't like it.

The guard was dressed head-to-toe in black, just like the guards on the videos. The gun was the same, too. An assault rifle.

'Get her the right I.D. next time,' he said, in an American accent.

Once we were well past the guard, I asked Gerald who owned the camp.

'It's complicated. Technically I think it's the French government. But the UK has a vested interest, so certain bits of it is under their jurisdiction. Like the security. We contracted that out to the Americans.'

'Why?'

'Because everyone here was trying to get to the UK or America. Old America, that is. The Worker programme has messed things up a bit, though. Now *New* America is where they want to be, above all, but it's the hardest place to get to. New America welcomes them, everyone else tries to stop them getting there. Who would do all our work, then, hmm? Old America runs the security, because, well, they can afford it, for one thing, but also because it gives them more say over who goes where. You said you wanted the toilet?'

He pointed at a long wooden fence that met some tents at the far end and stopped just in front of us. I looked at him.

'Behind there,' he said. 'Just, be careful where you tread. Don't touch anything.'

I walked up. The smell of sewage was so strong by the time I reached the fence that I gagged. I held my sleeve over my mouth and nose. I took a tentative step beyond the edge of the fence and looked round. Men, women, children - we were all using it at the same time. The children looked up at me, but the adults wouldn't make eye contact.

Men and boys were pissing up against the fence,

with nothing to drain it away at the bottom except the boggy grass. Women, girls and anyone who needed to sit down were perched over a long wooden bench, with a shallow seat, over a ditch. That's all it was. A ditch, running underneath everyone's back-end. I think there was supposed to be water running through it, to wash the waste away somewhere, but there wasn't. It all just piled up. The rain was landing in the mire, little pinpricks making the whole mass ripple, almost flicker.

I was vomiting, before I could move to do it over the ditch, I was bent over, throwing up on the grass. The smell and the sight just overwhelmed me. I stood, still bent, gasping, steadying myself with my hands on my thighs.

'Hey!' an angry voice shouted, just in front of me. I looked up, wiping my mouth with my sleeve. A woman who had been using the toilet stood with her arms folded, staring at me. 'Hey!' she said again, 'you a journalist?'

'No, I'm, I'm with the charity…'

'Where's your badge?'

'I don't have one, yet-'

'You come to gawp at us? Do we make you sick?' she asked, pointing at the pool of vomit near my feet.

'No, I'm… I'm not well, that's all, I-I want to help.'

'Help?' she asked, 'then where is the money. The papers. The transport. Hm? That's what we need. We don't need another grief-tourist staring at us, making us feel like fucking vermin. I'm old enough to be your mother. Jesus. At least journalists have cameras. They can let the world see what is going on. How are you going to help?' she asked.

'I… I don't know, yet…' I answered, weakly.

She shook her head and walked away.

'Ellie?' Gerald's voice called from behind the fence.

'Are you okay?'

No.

I emerged. I must have looked bad.

'What happened?' he asked, putting his hand on my shoulder. I flinched.

'I don't think I'm very well,' I said, watching a group of children playing in the walkway between one of the hundreds of rows of tents. They were kicking a scrunched-up paper ball around.

'I'm sorry,' he said, 'I put you in the deep end here. Do you want to go back?'

Home. Yes. I want to go back home.

'No. Yes. Well - I just need to use the bathroom. In our bit.'

He nodded. 'Come on.'

***

I had the first shower I'd had in days. The cubicle was next to the portaloo and it had the same smell. It was pretty dirty. I didn't care. It was nothing, compared to what I'd just seen. There was running water. There was soap.

I wrapped myself in the musty towel and tried my best to use the edges to squeeze the water from my hair. I was dreading stepping out into the cold. I was dreading going back into the camp even more. *You're in too deep.* Suddenly the door swung open in front of me.

'Shit!' I yelled, taking a step back. The cold rushed in.

'I'm sorry,' Dima said, 'I didn't think you'd be-'

'It's a shower,' I interrupted him, 'why didn't you knock?!'

'I did, you didn't hear,' he said, handing me something, 'I got you this, that's all.'

It was a waterproof jacket.

'Oh,' I faltered, 'thank you. How did you get it?'

'Doesn't matter.'

He turned and walked away.

'Thank you,' I called after him, 'really, thank you - I didn't mean to-'

He turned around, smiling, and shouted, 'It's okay. Get dry. You'll get cold.' Then he turned back and carried on.

Shit. I'm such a dick. I stood there, freezing, watching him walk back to the camp. I looked down at the coat in my hand. *Where did he get this from? How did he get it?* I thought of the people I'd seen using the toilets. *What happens in winter?* Nobody had a decent coat. Dima didn't, either.

Guilt. The guilt was overwhelming for the first few days. I knew it would be bad, but not that bad. I felt guilty asking about Anya. I felt like it made people doubt me, rightly. When I did ask about her, nobody recognised her name or description. I hadn't realised how useless I'd feel. Nothing I was doing would help. Not really. I felt like a fraud. I *was* a fraud. I was only fourteen, for a start. *Nearly fifteen*, I would tell myself, as though that made a difference. I had no money. I could only speak a bit of French and Spanish. I knew nothing about anything that mattered. I couldn't give answers to any of their questions. All I could do was give them the shitty supplies. Grey food. Grey bandages. Grey blankets. Grey soap, for the one semi-working shower between hundreds of people. The shower with a ragged curtain flapping about in the wind, with a notice stuck to it saying 'NOT DRINKING WATER' in five different languages. I was ashamed. Ashamed of how relieved I was to get away at the end of the day. How I would ache to get back to our tent, where there was dry bedding and clean water. How I would make things up to make the kids smile, even though I knew I was giving them false hope.

I borrowed Julia's phone to use her translate app. I'd hold it up and press the button when the kids spoke. It would tell me their questions. What's your name, where are you from, when can we leave?

'When are *you* leaving?' a little girl asked me.

I thought for a second. She was about Jake's age. She reminded me of him. The way she jumped about when she was excited, the way she fiddled with her sleeve when she was telling a story.

'I don't know,' I said to the phone, looking at her, 'why?'

She said something back. The purple line on the app rippled for a second, thinking, then the American voice spoke.

'Because everyone leaves us here, in the end.'

Chapter 6

'Next,' the woman said. She looked up at the man in the queue, who was staring at something in his hands. She said it again, in another language. He looked up.
She sighed, motioning for him to come and sit down.

Everywhere was so cold, except the assessment tent. It was full, all the time. There must have been hundreds of people under that battered tarpaulin - stood in the queue, sat on the floor, children running, weaving in and out of the line, finding games that didn't need words.

She was English, but I couldn't place her accent. Southern. Well-spoken. The government uniform was the same for men and women. A white shirt, grey blazer, grey trousers, black flat shoes. Black name badge. Hair had to be short or tied back. Hers was in a low bun. She opened her phone and spoke into the translator app, motioning to him to pass her the card in his hand.

'Which country are you wanting to work in?' she asked the app, reading the information on his card. She typed into her laptop. She still hadn't looked him in the eye.

He spoke as she held the phone up with one hand, typing with the other. His eyes flicked between her and the phone. It translated.

'UK. I have the papers.'

She put the phone down on the desk and typed faster. She scrolled through pages, scanning the screen.

Her eyes settled on something. Her face twitched. A slight wince, that she tried to hide. I could see it, though. So could he. He spoke. The phone buzzed into life.

'What is wrong?' the voice asked.

She finally looked at him. I knew what she was going to say.

'I'm sorry, Sir. You've been assessed as a Void.' The word sent a ripple through us all. It didn't need translation. Everyone within earshot stopped their conversation, their daydreaming, their dozing, to stare at the man. I gripped the bag I was carrying. It was my job to give out dextrose tablets and water to everyone in the queue, making sure nobody took more than one lot. I remembered the man from earlier in the day, in the middle of the queue. He'd insisted he didn't need anything, showing me his card, smiling. He thought the journey was over.

He shook his head, talking into the phone. She talked over him, reading his rights. She carried on with the script as he became more animated, standing up, gesturing back towards the queue, then her laptop, then himself. He was shouting. The phone had stopped trying to translate the competing voices. Her script came to an end.

'...no opportunity to appeal,' she finished, handing his card back.

He grabbed it, shouting still, and threw it on the floor.

'Sir, please don't become violent,' she said, glancing at the guard in the corner.

He shouted in English this time.

'My *life!* he shouted 'it is my *life*, my *family!* You are killing us,' he said, turning to point at the crowd behind him, looking back at her. 'You. You are killing us. Children. Children are dying.'

76

'Sir, there is nothing I can do,' she said, then leaned to see behind him and shouted 'next!'

He shook his head, shouting, 'no!' then lunged over the desk and grabbed her laptop, hurling it to the floor by the side of her. She jumped to the other side, one hand held up to shield her face. The guard was on him before he could turn around. She stood aside, pulling her shirt into place where it had runkled as she swerved. She smoothed her hair, watching the man being wrestled to the floor.

Nobody did anything. I did nothing. We just watched.

I watched the man's face as it was pressed against the floor, his wrists whiten as the cuffs tightened, his back arch as the guard pulled his head up to cover it with a spit-hood. The tent was quiet.

A noise startled me. She was plugging her laptop back in, settling back into her seat.

'Next!'

***

'You've only been here a few days, Ellie, don't worry.' Julia collected the mugs and plates from around the tent and handed them to Gerald, who had let the boiled water cool enough to wash them in the plastic tub that we used for everything.

'You get used to it. Remember, you're helping to make things better. You're not working for the government. You're one of the good guys, yeah?' she said, kneeling next to me. I sat on my bunk. I nodded. I didn't believe her, though.

'Why don't you call home, hm? It'll make you feel better.'

I wanted to cry. I nodded again.

'Use my phone. If you go over to the medical tent, that's where the best Wi-Fi is. Do a video call. You'll feel so much better, for seeing their faces.'

I got to the medical tent and stopped. It was one of those cold, clear nights where the darkness reaches into your lungs and makes you feel the night inside. The stars were all out. The camp was quite a long way out of the city, in the middle of requisitioned farmer's land. I stood, staring up at the sky. It looked like a deep purple dome, full of tiny holes in random patterns, letting light blaze through from a white fire behind. I closed my eyes, breathing in the night. *Go home*, I said to myself. *Just go home.*

'Ellie? Are you okay?'

I opened my eyes. It was Dima. He looked different in the moonlight. Black and white. Sepia. Superimposed into present day, from an old film. I realised I was smiling.

'No,' I said, 'but nobody here is, are they?'

I looked up at the stars again. I think he did the same.

'What happens to the refugees who are assessed as Voids?' I asked, turning to him.

He glanced at the floor, then looked up at me. His eyes were glassy.

'They wait. For a long time. Then they're sent back.'

'Back where?'

'To wherever they came from. Whatever they were running from. For most of them,' he looked at his feet as he kicked a stone away into the dark, 'it means death. It's a death sentence.'

His words hung in the air. I thought of the man I'd seen restrained, earlier. I thought of his face, the second before it was covered with the hood.

'Your name isn't Ellie, is it?' Dima asked, his voice

hushed.

I stared at him. *Shit.*

'It's Emma, right? Emma Morgan?'

I looked around. I don't know what I was expecting. Guards to wrestle me to the floor, maybe. Toma, Gerald, Julia, to come and bollock me. There was no one except us.

'How did you-' I whispered, then broke off as he produced a phone from his pocket.

'Your parents,' he said, unlocking the phone, 'they're looking for you.'

The blue-white light illuminated his face as he tapped and scrolled.

'What *the fuck*,' I said, 'I've only been gone for a few days, how did they?'

He handed me the phone. BBC News. *Shit. Shit shit shit.*

14-year-old girl missing after travelling to Dover

Police fear 14-year-old Emma Morgan may have attempted to cross the channel after she left home early on Tuesday morning. She told her parents that she was departing for a school trip to Berlin and would message them when she arrived. However, the school confirmed Emma never registered for the trip and was not present in their party upon departure.

CCTV tracked Emma travelling from Lulworth to Dover, alighting a National Express coach at approximately 10:40pm on Tuesday. The last confirmed sighting of Emma was this CCTV footage outside a private car park, where she appears to throw her phone away. Police are still trying to recover the phone, as the bin was emptied shortly after this footage was captured.

My vision swam. I handed the phone back, the rest of the

article unread. I sat down heavily on the wet grass, unable to bear my own weight in that moment.

Dima sat next to me.

'Why did you come here?' he asked.

'To find my friend.'

I wiped a tear off my cheek and sniffed, trying to hold back.

'Who is she?' he asked, shuffling in his pockets. He drew out a box of cigarettes and offered me one. I shook my head.

'Anya. She was in a Worker camp near my house. I used to go and see her. Just through the bars, at the back of the grounds. We were friends. She was there for a year. I went every week, sometimes every day. My brother loved her, too.'

'Why do you think she might be here?'

'Someone told me this is where the High-Risk Workers get processed.'

'Some do. But some of them go straight to Turkey. What was her last name?'

'I don't know… that sounds stupid doesn't it? After a year. But I don't. I just never asked her. She was just Anya. My friend.'

Fuck. I thought of Mum, Dad, Jake. What was I doing to them? I hadn't let myself really think about it until then. *Stop it. You'll disintegrate, right here on the grass, if you think about them.*

'I will have one, actually,' I said, watching him light up his cigarette and take a drag. He smiled and passed me his.

'We'll share,' he said, 'these things are like gold dust.'

I sucked on the end of it and spluttered. He laughed.

'I don't smoke,' I coughed, 'in case you couldn't tell.'

'Why did you want one?' he asked.

'I thought it might help,' I said, tasting the bitter

residue for the first time. It didn't. He said nothing. *What do I do now?* I searched my mind.

'She's not here.'

His voice echoed. I knew he was right.

'So what do I do?' I asked.

'You came here to find her. She's not here. People are looking for you. You have two choices,' he said, taking a drag. I watched the ash glow amber at the end of the cigarette. I watched his lips cling to the filter, then release it as he breathed in. 'You tell people who you are, you go back home. Or,' he looked at me, 'you find her. But if you want to do that, you'll have to change. Change a lot.'

'Like what?'

'How many languages do you speak?'

'One. And a bit...'

'You need at least three. What about your ID?'

'I don't have any.'

'Nothing?'

'No.'

'How did you get here?'

'I hid in a lorry.'

'Okay,' he said, smiling, 'you might have *some* of what it takes, in that case.' He took another drag. 'You'll need fake papers, to smuggle yourself into the Worker Transits. Do you know what that means?'

I shook my head.

'You have to pass as a High-Risk Worker, then you'll be transported to the facility. That's probably where she is.'

I took a deep breath. *Say it.* 'She might not be there. She might not be anywhere.'

'What do you mean?' he asked.

'She might be dead. She could have died. In the fire.'

He looked at me.

'There was a fire,' I explained, 'at the Camp she lived

in. People died. We never found out who died and who was evacuated. Transported. Who was transported.'

He stubbed his cigarette out on the sole of his shoe. The sparks fell away onto the grass, then died.

'Well...if she's alive, she's in Turkey.'

We sat in silence. The air was damp now. *He must be cold.* I knew I was. I was trying to hold myself still, to stop my shoulders, arms, hands from shaking, to stop my lower jaw from bouncing.

'Is she worth it?' he asked.

I thought of Anya. Her fingers wrapped around the bars, blanching as she held on tight, ready for me to pull the twine. Her blanched, soft face against the rough, parched grass. Anya asked me about my family, my life. She wanted to know about my plans for the future. She wanted me to do the things she couldn't. She was always so kind to me, despite having nothing. I thought of the way she would insist on breaking the chocolate bars I brought her into two, or three, if Jake were there. The way she always knew what to say to make Jake laugh. The way she remembered the stupid things I said about our cat.

'But Jangles doesn't like milk,' I heard her voice say to Jake, when he was lecturing her about how to get a cat to do tricks, *'she likes scampi flavoured Nik-Naks. You'd need lots of them.'*

'Yes,' I said, 'she's worth it.'

He exhaled.

Don't think about them, I told myself. *Don't think about Jake. Think about Anya. Alone. Who knows what she's going through? Worse than this.* I thought of the man being wrestled to the floor in the assessment tent. The woman who confronted me in the toilets. The little girl who knew I would leave.

'Okay,' he said, 'I can help.'

***

I lay awake that night, thinking about the news. *How long until someone recognises me?* The photo they'd used was a good one, luckily, and right then, I looked terrible. There was just one mirror in the charity worker's quarters. I didn't like to look at myself in it, but I did, after I saw the news report. I looked older. Tired. Pale. Grey. I was thankful for my mum. I knew it was her. Pride, vanity, insecurity - whatever it was, it meant she'd given them the one photo of me where I looked nothing like *the reality* of me.

About a year ago, at my cousin's wedding, I was a bridesmaid. My cousin was a semi-professional ballroom dancer and had a very specific idea for how us bridesmaids should look: spray tan, big hair, vibrant make-up. I thought I looked nothing like me. I had no idea how Dima recognised me from the photo. Looking back, maybe the two versions of me weren't so different, but at the time, I felt like Mum had unwittingly thrown a proper decoy out there for me. Maybe it did buy me some time.

I was thankful we were in a place with no TV and patchy Wi-Fi. Nobody seemed to pay much attention to the news, anyway - we were all in this awful parallel universe together, cut off. I pictured a press conference, my Mum crying, Dad trying not to. I wanted to let them know I was okay, but there was no way I could do that without being taken home. Anya had nobody to take her home, no home to go to. *She needs me.*

I spent the next day convinced everyone was looking at me differently. I was sure they knew, or suspected. Especially the government workers. Of course, they didn't. If they had, I would've been on the first boat back. A fourteen-year-old who smuggled herself into an Assessment Camp without her parents' knowledge? Wouldn't look good. They wanted to give the impression they had the situation tightly controlled. All on their terms. For the majority, that was true. Except for Dima. He seemed to get around things, somehow.

He appeared at the entrance of the medical tent, when I was supervising a group of children brushing their teeth, with the toothbrushes everyone had to share. Thankfully, they were too young to realise how grim that was. They were excited to be doing something different. Some of them weren't thorough enough, so I demonstrated with my finger, because I was too squeamish to use one of the shared brushes - another thing that made me feel guilty.

There were six children in front of me, all from different places. None of us spoke the same language. Alina had black hair and green eyes, like Dima. Ivan had mousey brown hair and grey eyes. Leo had red hair and hazel eyes. Yasmin, Damilola and Sunday had black hair and dark brown eyes. Everyone's skin was a different colour. There were more refugees from Africa and Central Asia, definitely, but also Eastern Europe. A few were from East Asia, but they tended to be processed faster, Gerald told me, because of the agreement between our governments.

I squeezed the tiniest amount of toothpaste onto my finger and held it up, pointing to their brushes and gesturing them over, holding the toothpaste ready. They crowded round, holding their brushes steady while I added blobs of paste. The ones who had a better technique than me would still watch me do it, because they were bored. We all were.

'Ellie!' Dima shouted. I looked up. He beckoned me over.

I scanned the tent for help.

'Toma?' I called. He was doing paperwork.

'Hm?'

'Could you take over for me? I have an urgent phone call from home,' I lied.

He put down his pen and walked over.

'Sure. Hope it's nothing bad.'

I wiped the toothpaste on my jeans and walked over to Dima. I knew he had a plan. I felt sick. It wasn't just waiting to hear the plan, though. I felt weird every time I saw him. Kind of light-headed. Nervous. Awkward.

'Come with me,' he said, walking off towards the toilet block as soon as I got near him.

The smell was worse. Even though it was cold, a sunny day made a difference. Intensified the odour. I tried to breathe through my mouth and closed off my soft palate, so I didn't have to cover my nose. He looked around. Nobody was near.

'I can get you into the Worker Transit. As a High Risk. If that's what you want.'

'Really? How?'

He pulled some papers from under his jacket, then put them back inside.

'Where did you get them?' I asked. 'How-'

'It's all trade,' he said, quietly, 'I've been doing this for months. I get things people want. Trade them for the things I want. It's not hard, if you know what you're doing.'

'How old are you?' I asked, without realising I was saying it out loud.

'Sixteen. Just. You're fifteen tomorrow, right?'

I paused.

'I don't know - what's the date? I don't even know what day of the week it is.'

'It's Tuesday,' he smiled, 'and you're fifteen

tomorrow, on the 14th.'

I held my face in my hands and took a deep breath.

'Shit. I don't know what's going on with me. How did you know?'

He hesitated.

'It was on the news, wasn't it?' I asked, feeling tears rise behind my eyes. I tried to swallow them back down.

He nodded. It was useless. A tear sprang up and fell down my face. I swiped at it, as though it was a fly that I could just get rid of.

'I'm sorry,' he said, putting his hand on my shoulder.

What am I doing? I asked myself. *What the fuck?*

'You don't have to do this,' he said, 'you can still go home. You don't even have to give up on her. You can find her through the authorities-'

'-Bullshit' I interrupted him.

He laughed.

'Okay, maybe not. But I could find her for you, you know? I have nothing to lose. You have everything.'

I wanted to kiss him, in that instant. We stood in a cesspit, in the seventh circle of hell, and all I wanted to do was kiss him.

'Dima!' a voice shouted. It was Gerald.

'I'll be at the medical tent tonight - after lights out,' he whispered, watching Gerald walk up the pathway. I nodded.

'Dima, you should be in the other section. You know that,' Gerald said, shaking his head, out of breath from his hurried pace. 'Go on, run. If you're not there for the rollcall you know what will happen.'

'I'm going,' he said, catching my eye before he turned and jogged away.

We watched him turn the corner and disappear. Gerald turned and looked at me. He looked like my dad did, when he found me on the path down the side of the house. Angry and scared at the same time.

'He's a charmer, that boy,' he said, 'but don't let him get under your skin. He's not a bad kid, but he's mixed up in some bad things. I'm sure he doesn't mean any harm… but they never do, do they?'

The sun was setting. We walked back in silence. I had no answer for him. *You're too late*, I thought.

In our tent, I flinched. I looked at my finger. It was bleeding. I'd peeled some of my skin off, by mistake. I was making my way through a pile of carrots, staring at the floor just in front of me as I dragged the peeler over the rough orange surface.

'Ow,' I said, sucking the tip of my finger.

'Let me see,' said Julia, moving my hand next to the lamp.

'Ooh. That's nasty. Here, let me bandage it up.'

She rifled through a box under her bunk. I stared back at the same patch of floor as before.

'Are you okay?' she asked, taking my hand again, swabbing an antiseptic wipe over my finger.

'I'm fine. Just tired.'

She wrapped the bandage around my finger and snipped across the width with scissors. She motioned for me to hold it in place so she could cut some tape. I held it.

'Dima is such a nice kid,' she said.

I looked at her.

'I'm not blind,' she said. 'Gerald isn't, either.'

She cut the tape and stuck down the bandage. I felt my face flush and wished I'd paid better attention peeling the carrots.

I felt like saying: *you're not my mum. Gerald's not my dad. I can look after myself.* But I didn't. Partly because I didn't believe it. They were my parents, in the camp. And a loud voice in my head insisted that I was doing a very shit job of looking after myself.

'You have a good life to go back to,' she said, leaning with her elbows on her knees and her chin resting on her hand. 'Don't get attached. It will make it so much harder to leave at the end of the summer.'

I nodded.

'You're worth more to us, to them, doing a good job while you're here, yeah? He's a good kid. But you know he's fucked, right? I mean, he's in this place. He's not a volunteer. He's a refugee.'

It startled me. I'd never heard Julia swear before.

'I know, I know,' I said, 'I know he is.' *I don't care though*, I thought.

'He's a Void, too. You knew that, didn't you?'

I looked at her.

'What?'

She took a deep breath.

'He's a Void. Dima. I'm not surprised he didn't tell you. Honestly, the only thing he has in front of him is a long, torturous wait. Then what? A journey, first. If he survives that, then, well, the only thing waiting for him at the other end is-'

'-Don't,' I interrupted her. I couldn't let her say it. To make it real. 'Don't say it. I know, alright, I know what's waiting for him.'

Chapter 7

I'd had the same nightmare every night since being in Calais. I'm outside the back of Lulworth, where we used to meet Anya, at night. It's dark, but I know she's coming to see me, so I wait, trying to keep warm. Jake isn't there. I'm so cold, I decide I have to light a fire. I make one just by crashing two stones into one another. The sparks settle on the twigs and engulf them, immediately.

I'm watching the door Anya is supposed to come through, waiting, stretching my hands out near the flames to warm them. She appears, behind the window in the door, but as soon as she sees me she screams. I turn to see the fire has spread over the moorland behind me.

The whole hillside is ablaze. I'm trapped. I need to get into the facility, but I'm stuck behind the fence. I try to climb it. Anya runs out and reaches up to pull me over to her side of the fence, to safety. But the flames are licking at my back and around my shoulders now, the smoke is drowning me. She reaches through the bars, nesting her hands to give me a foot-up, but the fire grabs her. Suddenly I'm being lifted, from behind, I can't see who or what is doing it but I'm being dragged up and away, watching the flames take hold of Anya as she falls to her knees. I'm screaming, wrestling with the invisible force dragging me up and back, to get down to her, but it's useless. That's when I wake up.

I had the same nightmare that night, with something

new. When Anya catches fire, Dima appears in the doorway and runs to her to try to put out the flames. He can't see me. Only Anya. I watch him try to smother the flames with his jacket, but it doesn't work. He's coughing, choking, just like her. I'm shouting at them to go back inside for help, but they can't hear me. It's too late. They're both burning now. They're dying, and I'm watching them die.

I woke with a thrash. Trying to free myself in the dream spilled over into the reality of throwing my blanket off. Guilt clawed at my ribs. I hadn't gone to meet Dima. I was too scared. Scared of whatever his plan was, yes, but more than that. I was scared to look at him. Scared to be around him, now I knew what was going to happen to him.

What Julia told me, just hours before, changed everything.

The terror-sweat that spread over my neck and back while I slept had cooled. I shivered. Julia shifted. I kept my watch in a concealed inside pocket of my rucksack, after Gerald insisted I couldn't wear it in the camp, so I tapped the screen of Julia's phone on the floor to check the time. 2am. *Dima will have gone. Ages ago.* I got up, anyway. I thought maybe I could find him, wherever he was. I felt as though the nightmare was a sign that I had to check that he was okay, after I didn't show up.

For once, it was the temperature you'd expect for a midsummer night. I wasn't shivering. After I'd walked down there, I didn't even need my jacket.

The guard stood aside as I flashed my badge. He knew me now. He never gave eye contact, though. I wanted to ask him why he did this job. Why he was here, so far from home, bullying others who were so far from theirs. I made up histories for all of them, the guards. The one on the gate was angry with the world because he'd been cheated on by his first girlfriend, who he'd loved since he was six years old. The one in the assessment tent was an out-and-out psychopath who tortured animals when he was a kid. The one in the medical tent didn't want to be there, he *hated* being there, but he had to do this job, because it was the only way he could afford to pay for his mum's cancer treatment.

I made my way through the dark warren. I could smell smoke. I began to walk faster. *There's a fire.* I searched for a glow, for sparks rising above the canopies. I thought I could see something, smoke, drifting up from behind the next tent. I started running. I could see the people on the roof at Lulworth, waving for help, trying to climb down the side of the building, falling. *This time, I will help.* I turned the corner and smacked into someone in the dark. Dima.

'Shit!' I said, stumbling backwards. In that second, I realised what I'd thought was a fire was just the smoke from his cigarette. 'Fucking hell,' I muttered, half laughing, half genuinely swearing.

'Are you okay?' he asked, looking confused.

'Yes. Sorry, I'm fine. I just - I thought there was a fire. The smoke,' I said, gesturing towards the cigarette. I shook my head. 'I'm losing it.'

'Is that why you came?'

'No. I came to see you. To find you.'

I could see he didn't believe me. He looked at the floor.

'I've been here for hours,' he said, dropping the cigarette end on the floor and smothering it into the grass with his foot. He laughed, shaking his head. 'I don't know why I'm still here-'

I kissed him.

I felt as though I'd left my body, somehow. I was there, but I wasn't there. Like I was watching it happen. I could see his arm move, see his palm against the small of my back, see his fingers touching the fabric of my T-shirt. My hand on the back of his neck, my fingers in his hair. His eyelashes, casting shadows as he closed his eyes. It was a soft kiss. I was bold enough to get there, but somehow caught off guard once I had. I pulled away.

'Sorry,' I said, quietly, 'I didn't know what to say, so…'

I watched the grass in the dark. I was struggling to look him in the eye. I couldn't quite believe I'd done it. He grabbed my hand and I finally looked up. He smiled.

'It said what you needed to say,' he laughed, then gently lifted my hand and kissed my fingers. I smiled, shaking my head.

'Don't say it again, though,' he added, pressing my hand then loosening his grip, letting go, his smile fading. I stopped still. *What?*

'What do you mean?' I asked, feeling a wave of nausea run up my body.

'I'm a Void. I didn't tell you. We're the lowest of the low.'

He closed his eyes and rubbed his eyelids. *Is that? Is he crying?*

'I know,' I said, putting my hand on his arm, 'Julia told me, I know, don't worry.'

He looked up. There were tears, but he thumbed them away.

'Then you're stupid,' he said, pulling the papers out of his jacket. 'You don't know what it means, really. Here - take these,' he held the papers out, his hand shaking. 'Ignore me from now on. I'm sorry. Good luck, you'll need it.'

He turned and walked away.

'What the fuck?' I called after him, 'Hey! Wait!'

I ran after him. He stopped.

'I know what it means, okay?' I said, 'that's why I didn't come. Julia told me and I was terrified.'

He stood, listening, letting the tears fall. The moonlight showed just a hint of the bloodshot through the whites of his eyes. The rest was dark. The green had merged with the black. His eyes reminded me of a deer's. The only one I'd ever seen close up. One ran out in front of us in the dark when dad was driving once, down a dual carriageway. I thought we'd crashed into another car, a wall, even, the impact was so hard. I remember freaking out about Jake, seeing his car seat jolt forwards and his head do the same, snapping back too fast. He immediately started crying, though, and asking to get out, which was a relief. After we pulled over, dad spotted where the deer had ended up. It was lying on the embankment, thirty yards back, facing the other way. The car was a write-off. The deer was lying still. I ran up to it, ignoring mum shouting after me to stop. She was carrying Jake. Dad was on his phone to the breakdown service. I stopped a couple of feet away. The deer looked grey in the dark, except for its muzzle and the tips of its ears. They caught the light. I could see its flank rise and fall. Still breathing. I made my way slowly round to the front of her and knelt down. She looked at me but didn't move. Her eyes were deep, black, full of something more than they showed. Like water rushing at the bottom of a crevasse. You can only see a snapshot of it as it moves, but you know it comes from somewhere, and it's going somewhere else. Dima's eyes were the same.

'I can't do it,' he said, wiping his eyes, 'I can't.'

'Do what? What do you mean?'

'Fall in love with you.'

I didn't know what to say. How to look, what to do with my body. How to breathe. I was breathing too fast. My heartbeat was too loud in my ears, I felt like he could hear it.

'I'm…' I started, not knowing how I was going to finish the sentence, 'I'm… not asking you to do that…'

'No,' he shook his head and smiled. 'You're not. But I like you. And if you like me, like it felt like you did when you kissed me, just now, you're going to get hurt.'

'Fuck that!' I said, then tried to collect myself, pacing up and down the grass, taking deep breaths, thinking.

Searching my mind, but nothing was coming. I looked up at the sky. *Think.* I could feel him stood there, watching me.

'You got me these papers,' I said, finally, holding them up, 'and this jacket,' I pointed to the coat I'd thrown on the floor. He wouldn't look me in the eye. 'You get cigarettes. You've got a phone, from somewhere. You sneak into our quarters, into the government quarters. You get what you need. All of this, despite being a Void.' Finally he looked up at me. 'I'm fifteen,' I carried on, 'I don't speak any languages. I don't even have a fucking phone. I know nothing about the world, except that it's wrong and I want to make it right somehow, but I don't know where to start. I need you. Right?'

I came to the realisation as I was talking. I looked at him differently. He was more to me than some guy I'd kissed in a moment of madness. He was my key to opening all the doors. The strand through the labyrinth that I could follow to Anya and bring us out alive again.

'I need you,' I said again, I'd never been more sure of anything. 'Look, I promise, I won't do anything like that again. I don't… love you, or anything like that, it was just the heat of the moment. That's all. Please. You have to help me.'

'How?' he asked. He knew I was right. I didn't stand a chance without him. He had nothing to lose. He was listening.

'Come with me. Through the Worker Transit.'

'I don't know, I can't just-'

'-Why not?' I interrupted. 'What's keeping you here?'

'Nothing, except them,' he said, nodding towards the government quarters. A smile started to make its way across his face.

'Come on,' I urged him, 'do you think I stand the remotest chance of finding Anya without you?' I asked.

'You got here on your own,' he said, 'don't underestimate yourself.'

I wasn't going to answer that. I waited.

'Okay,' he said, smiling, 'fuck it. Why not. I was only waiting here to be deported anyway. Maybe I'll just deport myself.'

I hugged him, then remembered myself and pulled away.

'Sorry,' I said, 'sorry. Thank you. Thank you so much.'

He smiled and shook his head. I think he couldn't quite believe what was happening. Neither could I, but I was wide awake. I wanted to go. Suddenly, it all seemed possible, in a way I'd never really believed it was before.

'What do we do now then?' I asked.

'I need papers for me, too. I don't know how fast I can get them. The next Worker Transit to the High-Risk Facility is tomorrow... we might make it. I'll-'

'Ellie!' hissed Julia's voice. We spun around to see Julia coming fast down one of the walkways towards us.

'Shit. I'll meet you tomorrow,' I said, picking up my coat and hiding the papers under it.

He vanished. I turned to see him walk off, but he was gone.

'Ellie!' she said again, grabbing my arm as she reached me. I pulled away, instinctively. She sought my eye line and stared at me.

'I'm not your mother, but if I were, I would want you to go home. You need to go home, Emma.'

Emma? I felt my legs buckle. I stumbled and had to hold her arm to steady myself.

'What… how-'

'You're on the news. Missing from Lulworth. Emma Morgan. They think you tried to make your way to Calais. Well, they were right, weren't they? You're here. What *the fuck* is going on, Ellie? Emma. Whatever your name is. It's only because of the bureaucracy between all the competing agencies in places like this that they haven't started searching *over here* yet.'

I was too terrified to talk. She dragged my arm and I walked alongside her, stumbling through the dark, my trainers screeching against the wet grass.

***

'What would you do, if you were me, hm?' Julia asked.

She sat on her bunk, opposite me. Gerald was doing the night shift down at the arrivals section. It was just me and her.

I knew what I'd do. I'd call my mum.

'I don't know,' I said, 'I want to let them know I'm okay but I can't… I just can't give up on her, she's alone… suffering-'

'-How do you know? You don't even know if she's alive, Emma.'

'I just do. I can feel it. I know she's alive and I know she needs help. She could be in one of those awful facilities, starving… she could have been trafficked into sex work, anything-'

'-let's say that were true,' said Julia, putting her hands up, as though it would calm me down. 'Say she's being held in a cellar by a Romanian gang. What can you do about it?'

'Don't be flippant, she's-'

'No, I'm not being flippant. I'm being serious. What are you going to do? A fourteen-year-old-'

'-fifteen.'

'Whatever. A fifteen-year-old girl. Do you have any idea what you could be up against? The best you can hope for is that the authorities get a hold of you and take you home. The closer to the UK they find you, the better. Because the further you get, the less they care about how they treat you, yeah? That's the *best-case scenario*. More likely, you'll end up dead.' She fixed my gaze. 'That's me being serious. Completely serious. Remember when those kids were on the news for going off to join Islamic State? And the other ones were on the news for going off to fight them? This is the same. They all died in the end. Except one, who will live in limbo for the rest of her life.'

'This is nothing like that! I just want to get my friend home-'

'I'm sorry, Ellie - Emma,' she shook her head, 'I have to tell them. You'll hate me for it now, but it might just save your life.'

And just like that, I felt it all fall down. The walls of the fortress I'd been building started to collapse. The fizz of excitement, adrenaline, that had kept me going this whole time, burned out. Dread was all that replaced it. I was being dragged down a deep, dark, cold tunnel. Clawing at the walls, my fingers bleeding. Dragged back home, back to school, back to letting it all happen and doing nothing to stop it. Back to not knowing the worst of it. Maybe I was better off before, but now I'd seen behind the curtain, I couldn't go back. Not until I'd found her.

I didn't say anything. I knew Julia had made her mind up. She got up and rummaged in her rucksack, retrieving her toothbrush. I watched her do her bedtime things. I was so still. I felt my frame creak with each breath.

'Get some sleep,' she said, climbing into her bunk, 'I'm going over there first thing. They'll have a lot of questions for you. They might even take you back tomorrow. It will be a long day, whatever happens.'

I got in bed. She turned out the light as I lay back. I stared up at the roof. The moon was bright enough to mean it wasn't really dark. The light glowed through the thin, beige tarpaulin enough for me to be able to see the outline of my fingernails as I held my hands in front of my face. I listened to the sounds from the camp. It was never really quiet, even in the early hours. There was always someone awake. Something going on. People talking. Food being prepared. Clothes being washed. New arrivals to be processed. Arrests to be made.

I would miss the smell of our tent. It reminded me of childhood. Camping. Sleeping bags, Gore-Tex boots, Calor Gas, waterproof lining. I went missing once, before, as a child. When we went on a camping holiday, down to Devon. Before Jake was born. I woke up in the middle of the night, bored. Everyone was asleep, so I decided to go for a walk. I must've been four or five, I think. I decided to go back to where we'd been that day, because I remembered it was fun. I was sure I knew the way. It was dark, but the moon was out. Up the hill, over the fence, down the slope. There was a hedge, running along the perimeter of the field, full of blackberries. I remember thinking, *I'll go and pick some more*. Getting over the style on my own was an effort, but I did it. I looked down the hill and saw the hedge, waiting there in the dark for me. I was proud. I thought of how impressed everyone would be the next morning when I showed them my stash of fruit. I would tell them the fairies put them there, by my sleeping bag, in the night. That's what the smell of the tent made me think of.

I looked at Julia. Her dreadlocks were plaited, draped over her shoulder. Her mouth was slightly open. Every now and then a faint wheeze escaped it. That usually meant she was properly asleep. I coughed, then closed my eyes, pretending to be asleep, listening for movement, a break in her breathing pattern. Nothing. I opened them and coughed again. She didn't stir.

Okay. Let's do this.

Chapter 8

'Don't speak,' he said, 'let me do the talking, okay?'

I nodded. I knew a few phrases, the ones he'd taught me, just now. We sat leaning against the back of an old stone cattle trough, long dried up, in the field behind the bus shelter, for an hour. The air was cold and clear, dew settled on the grass. The sun had been rising for a while, still casting long shadows. The pastel pink sky was shifting to blue, only broken by vapour trails from planes, here and there.

I sat there, breathing it in, wishing Anya were with us. And Jake. We'd enjoy doing things that Jake would enjoy, because it was an excuse to be a kid again. Make daisy chains. Do cartwheels and handstands. Go and feed the donkeys in the next field. Misha wouldn't do things like that. She wanted to do makeovers. Make films on our phones where we re-enacted her favourite music videos. Go hang out forever down at Park Gardens because Jensen McAndrew was always there and she was obsessed with him.

It all seemed so far away now. If you'd have told me, the girl awkwardly drinking cider that I didn't want just to fit in down at Park Gardens, pretending to be interested in Jensen's friend's skateboard, that this summer I would traffic myself abroad to an Assessment Camp, then try to smuggle myself into a High-Risk Facility - I'd have said you were out of your mind. But there I was.

Dima said he knew I was in trouble when Julia came to get me, so he'd followed us back to the tent. He listened outside. Once he knew she was planning to turn me in, he went back, got his things, stole papers from a High-Risk teenager due to leave next week, then came back. He was there, waiting for me, when I snuck out. We cut a hole in the fence right next to my tent. I sometimes wonder how things might have gone if he'd not followed me that night.

Dima told me Russian was the best cover for me, because there were a few countries where they spoke it and I looked like I could be from any one of them, too. My papers didn't specify my nationality. Once you were assessed as High Risk, it didn't matter. You were in a category all of your own. Not completely stateless, like a Void, but your only affiliation was to the Worker category. As a Worker, you could work anywhere that signed up to the scheme. Mostly western countries. Except for the ones who took a stand against it, like New America.

It would only work if I never had to speak it, though, because I could barely say a word. Dima taught me the Russian for *My name is Yulia, I don't understand, yes, no, thank you, please.* That was it. I repeated them to myself over and over, out loud. My pronunciation was so bad, Dima ended up laughing at me. As long as he could just tell people I was Russian, if they asked, we might be okay.

People started to congregate at the bus stop. I could feel my imaginary idyll slipping away as it filled with voices, bags, sadness. Nobody waiting wanted to be there. When there were enough people, we stood up and wandered around the corner, merging into the crowd. I fiddled with my bracelet, watching everyone in the rising sunlight. I decided to remove the ribbon. *What's the point of hiding Anya's tooth, now?* It made me feel better, seeing that part of her was with me. I bent down and picked a daisy, then tied the red ribbon around the stem in a bow. I put it in the cattle trough, hoping a kid like Jake would find it and smile.

Everyone started gathering their things. I looked up the road and saw a bus coming towards us. I took a deep breath and hauled my rucksack back on. I hadn't worn it since the night I arrived. I thought of the lorry driver. His silhouette above me, then his body on the floor of the trailer by my feet. *He was breathing*, I told myself. *He started moving. You saw it.*

The crowd gathered around the bus as it drew up. Out stepped a guard. He shouted instructions in French. I followed Dima's lead. We stood in a line, papers in hand. The guard motioned for the first in the queue to board. He took her papers and tapped something into his tablet. He handed the papers back, then stepped aside for her to get on.

'These are all High Risk, then?' I whispered, watching her step up onto the bus.

'Yes. Don't speak.'

I looked back at the fence. Two fields stretched between where we were waiting and the camp. I couldn't see anyone there, but I knew it wouldn't be long. It was coming up to 6:30am. If she hadn't already, Julia would wake up soon and realise I was missing. She'd go outside and see the hole in the fence. She'd report it and they'd start searching for me.

I watched the crowd slowly filter through into the bus, like sand through an hourglass. Then I saw two figures by the fence, up at the camp. Near the big tear. *Shit.* I couldn't tell who they were, but they were inspecting the damage.

I must have been tapping my foot, bouncing my knee, pacing, something, because Dima put his hand on my arm and said, quietly but firmly, *calm down*. We were the second to last to approach the bus. Everyone moved slowly. Nobody wanted to get on, except me. I looked at Dima as he handed over our papers. *Does he want to be here?*

The guard said something to the driver, who looked at us both, then said something back. They weren't speaking French. It was a language I didn't recognise. Dima didn't, either. I could tell. The guard swiped through his tablet while the driver looked at us. *Shit. Shit, he knows who I am. He's looking up the news to find that photo. Maybe they've all been emailed about me. He's searching for it. So,* I thought, *this is the man who will take me home.* I didn't want to go with him. *I should have listened to Julia.*

The guard finished tapping and looked up at us. He motioned with a nod of his head for us to get on. I struggled to hide my relief. I felt like laughing. We took off our backpacks and carried them on. We got as near to the back of the bus as we could, to be as far away from the guard and driver as possible.

'Remember,' Dima said as we sat down, 'we're still in France. Don't get used to it.'

'To what?'

'A rack for your bag, Seats, windows.'

'Are you okay being here?' I asked, watching him survey the interior. Since we emerged on the other side of the fence, I'd not been able to shake the feeling that he was angry with me. Maybe angry is too strong - annoyed. Irritated by me. Resentful, maybe.

He looked at me, then half-smiled.

'I'm fine. Like you said, it's not like I have anything back there.'

We both looked out of the bus window at the camp. The people who were inspecting the fence before had gone. The engine of the bus started. Dima was nervous.

Maybe even more than me. He knew what we were in for, that's why. Ignorance was bliss, for me. All I cared about was getting away.

The driver said something to the guard, who stood at the front and addressed everyone in French. He said we would be in Hungary by around midday tomorrow. There would not be many stops. Smoking was not allowed on the bus. I couldn't translate the rest. Something about checkpoints. Dima shifted in his seat. The guard told the driver to proceed. I looked back at the camp, convinced I would see a police escort suddenly speeding down the slope towards us. Nothing. The bus pulled away. The next time we stopped, we would no longer be in France.

**

I woke, my neck stiff, shoulders aching. There was no air conditioning, but a small window halfway up the bus did open, which made the heat bearable when it was moving, at least. I took off the hoodie I'd fallen asleep in and saw the sweat patches under my arms. I could tell there would be one on my back, too. Out of the window, the farmland stretched away for miles, flat and beige. Every now and then a shed or a crumbling farmhouse broke the expanse. Telephone pylons. Road signs. I looked over at Dima. He was asleep. Just like the first time I saw him. He opened his eyes and saw me smiling. *Shit.* He didn't smile back, just closed his eyes and turned the other way.

Fuck. What a mess.

I took a deep breath and thought about Jake. *Please don't be ill. No more headaches.* Then I berated myself for thinking that, because of course he would feel ill, after this. Life would be one massive headache at home right now. I hoped Julia would let them know I was okay.

Surely, she has to. She'll tell the authorities. They'll pass it on. Maybe she'll contact mum through the Facebook campaign. She'll let them know. She has to.

They'd be on to me, though. If Julia told them I was looking for Anya, surely they'd know I was on my way to Turkey.

At the next checkpoint, I started to sweat more. The bus was still, so no air blew through the window. Instead it just hung there, thick with heat, the same air all our hot lungs were breathing in and out.

Dima didn't even wake up. The guard boarded and did the same thing they all did. Walked up and down the aisle, checking everyone's papers. *She knows,* I told myself, *she has a picture of me behind her desk and instructions to take me in.* I tried to slow my breathing as she reached our seats. She asked for the papers, in German. Dima stirred and sat up, reaching for his papers. I let him hand both of ours over. She looked at me, for a long time. Then at Dima. I swallowed. She asked him a question in a language that wasn't German. I don't know what it was. He answered. All I could do was watch. She nodded, then looked at me again. She asked me something. I opened my mouth to try 'I don't understand' in Russian, but Dima interjected. Whatever he said was enough, and she handed the papers back.

I waited until she had left the bus and we were on the move again to ask Dima what had happened.

'She wanted to know why we were travelling together.'

'What did you say?'

'I said we were cousins. The only ones left alive, from a big family.'

'Wow. That's… grim.'

'Nah. They're used to it.'

'Who?'

'The guards. Wherever you are, the security have heard it all before. Workers almost always have something like that happen, it's why they're Workers. Not always, but a lot. The High-Risk ones are more likely to have come from a war zone. They're more likely to have lost all their family. It makes us volatile.'

'So you were a High Risk before, then?' I said, under my breath.

He nodded.

'High Risks have done something, been involved in something, that makes them more likely to pose a threat than your average Worker. All Workers are running from something. Poverty, mainly. Persecution. War. But it's all relative, you see. You can flee a warzone before anything bad happens to you. Then, maybe, you aren't so messed up. Or you can stay...until the bitter end.'

I watched his eyes fix on the back of the seat in front. I wanted to ask him what happened. Why was he High Risk? What tipped him over into being a Void? I couldn't ask him. I'd already got him into this mess. He was quiet. He avoided my eyes, and I didn't blame him.

Mile after mile, I felt the weight grow heavier and heavier. Every road sign we passed, every checkpoint we sat through, dragged me down. He barely spoke. *He hates me, I thought. Hates me so much.*

Why are you surprised?

I felt alone. *You've been kidding yourself, about Dima.* I leaned my head on the window and watched the darkness fall over the fields. The cool draft from the window brushed the side of my face. I traced the black rubber seal with my finger. *You're on your own. You don't even know what country you're in. The language you're supposed to speak. The reason you're supposed to give for being here. Sort yourself out.*

Nobody else is going to.

***

'Emma!' I heard Dima's voice, quiet, but sharp.

I opened my eyes. Daylight. Another checkpoint. I stretched.

'Where are we?' I asked.

'The border with Hungary. The Hungarian guards are worse than the Austrian ones.'

'Which are they?' I asked, looking at the two men in uniform boarding the bus. Dima's face told me the answer. They looked like the guards at the camp. All in black. Assault rifles. Stab vests. Steel cap boots.

The first guard eyed everyone, while the other collected in papers. The first asked one of the women in the front row a question. I recognised her. It was the woman who had confronted me in the toilet area at the camp. He shouted something at her. I felt everyone shrink back into their seats, suddenly quiet. She had no answer for him. He grabbed her arm and hauled her up out of the seat. Her friend tried to pull her back, but the other guard intervened. She was removed from the bus. I felt Dima tense up, next to me. His eyes were fixed on the space just to the right of the door, below the window. The guard pushed the woman against the side of the bus in that exact spot. We felt her body hit the metal. He was shouting at her. Still, she had no answer. He lifted the but of his gun above her, shouting still. She said something, crying. He brought it down, sharp and fast, against her temple. She fell. Dima stood up, straining to see her. Suddenly he was gone. I turned to see the other guard dragging him off the bus.

His eyes caught mine and he shook his head, just in time to stop me screaming 'no!' My guts were in knots. I watched him outside, desperate for him to come back. His hands were up, palms facing the guard. He was talking quietly, slowly, making sure not to look at the woman on the floor. I realised someone was addressing me, from the aisle. I glanced to see the driver, talking to me. I had no idea what language he was speaking. *Shit. He's asking a question. You'll have to do it.*

'Ya- ya-' I stammered, 'ya nye po-nee-ma-yoo' I tried.

He frowned. *Fuck.* He asked me a question in a different language to the first. Was he speaking Russian? I realised I was breathing too fast. I was hot. Too hot. I was going to be sick. I rushed past him, holding my hand over my mouth. I stumbled down the stairs and barely made it off the bus before I let it all out, spewing bile all over the grass verge. I gasped. *Think. Sorry. What was 'sorry'?*

I looked up. Everyone was watching me. The woman who had been hit was getting to her feet. She looked relieved. Dima looked like he was trying not to laugh. The guards looked irritated, but my display had broken whatever the situation was. We were all rounded back up onto the bus. The driver stopped me on the way back to my seat. He turned and reached up into the compartment above us. I swallowed, my legs feeling unsteady. He handed me a paper bag, gesturing to use it if I needed to vomit again. I exhaled, nodding.

Once we were through the border, Dima turned and smiled at me.

'Thank you,' he said, 'you got us out of that one.'

I shrugged and nearly laughed. It was almost funny. It would have been funny if it didn't feel like we were all about to die.

'What happened?' I asked.

'Oh, he was just throwing his weight around, that's all.'

'No, I don't mean back there. I mean, with you.

What happened to make you…' I lowered my voice, 'High Risk… a Void?'

He took a deep breath.

'I'm from Syria,' he said, 'that probably tells you all you need to know.'

It didn't. All I knew was that the country was ruined by war. There were lots of refugees. But most of them ended up being Workers, not Voids. As far as I knew, anyway.

'Do you have… is there anyone to go back to?'

'No,' he said, straight away, firmly. 'No-one. I'm going to get some sleep before we get to the train station. It's old trains, from there.'

He closed his eyes and turned away from me. Alone again.

I wanted to ask him about the next leg of the journey. *Old trains*. What did that mean, exactly? All the way from Budapest to Turkey. That would be a long, long time on a train. An *old* train.

I wished I could brush my teeth. The acid from the sick felt as though it was stripping the enamel from them. My tongue felt furry. I watched the villages roll by and couldn't quite believe how far from Lulworth I was. Less than a week ago, I was packing my rucksack for a fake school trip. I felt as though years had passed since then. Julia's voice was in my head.

The closer to the UK they find you, the better. Because the further you get, the less they care about how they treat you, yeah?

Chapter 9

The bus drew up.

'Why are we stopping here?' I asked Dima.

'It's the station.'

I frowned. We were in the middle of nowhere, as far as I could see.

'We're not going to the one in Budapest?'

'You think they'd do all this, where the tourists are?' he asked, laughing. 'We'll pass through it. But you won't see it.'

I watched everyone get up and tried to ignore the dread gnawing in my stomach. A couple of single-storey timber buildings sat next to the platform, with a guard leaning against the archway that joined them. There was no sign naming the station. As we got off the bus, I scanned around for signs of life. There was a village in the distance. I could make out a church spire. Closer, just in the next field, there was one house with its shutters closed. It had yellow, stained walls and a brown pitched roof. A dog in the yard was watching us, sitting in the shade of a tree. It got up, paced the perimeter. A chain ran from his collar to a post, stuck in the ground, in the middle of the dirt. A guard dog.

'Come on,' said Dima, quietly. He looked sick. Scared.

'Are you okay?' I asked, as we made our way with

everyone through the arch.

'Don't speak while the guards are near,' he whispered.

I swallowed. Dima was pale, his face damp with sweat. I thought he might faint. I pulled him back from the edge of the platform and made him wait nearer the wall. He was watching the bend in the track, where it disappeared behind trees. We could hear the train coming for a long while before it appeared.

That's not ours. It's a freight train. A cattle train, maybe. There were no windows in the carriages. Grates, at the top, that was all. It slowed, finally reaching a stop right in front of us. I could smell manure, or something like it. Something sour. Dima looked like he was going to vomit. He swallowed. I watched his face and realised this *was* our train.

The guard was still leaning against the wall of the archway. Finally, he pushed himself off the wall and strolled over. We watched him pace the length of the train, watching the grates of each carriage as he passed. He shouted and banged on the wooden slats. Shouts, bangs answered back. We heard a scream from inside the last one. I caught the eye of a woman stood with us, the one who had been hit with the butt of a gun earlier. I wondered if she remembered me. If she did, she had more important things to worry about now. There was nothing we could say to each other, but we knew what the look we exchanged meant. The guard thumped the next carriage. No reply. He shouted up at the grates. Nothing. Then he called up to us, beckoning.

Nobody moved. He barked something, putting his hand on the gun that hung at the top of his thigh. We started a slow shuffle up the platform. Dima took deep breaths. I decided to do the same. The woman's skin was starting to bruise, where she'd been hit. A small graze

over a purple-green blush. I watched her looking at the
guard. Different uniform, same story. She didn't look
scared. She looked angry. I felt it radiating from her. I
could feel, she wanted to throw him under the next train
to thunder past. I wished we could both do it.

He hauled open the door of the carriage. No seats.
Straw. I could see straw on the floor. *It's for animals. Surely.*
It smelled like they had already been there. We were
herded on. *Fuck.* Once everyone was on board, there was
barely room to sit down. I got separated from Dima. He
was at the other end of the carriage. I was worried about
him. He wasn't right. I strained to catch sight of him but
there were too many people in the way. All I could see
was the back of his head.

We all turned to watch as the guard shouted
something, then shut the door. I heard him lock it. Some
light came through between the wooden slats, but it was
still dark. It was hot. I felt just the same as I did when I
realised I might be trapped in the lorry. I started
breathing too fast, unable to control it. I needed to get
out. The bodies, so many bodies all crowding in on me,
the heat and the smell and - I felt my heart thudding so
fast, tight pain across my ribs, collarbone. As though
someone was sitting on my chest. I couldn't breathe. *I'm
having a heart attack*, I remember thinking, very clearly, *this
is a heart attack. I'm going to die.* Then nothing.

***

I could hear someone saying my name. It wasn't Dima,
though. I opened my eyes and saw her face.

'I'm Aminah,' she said, 'we've met before.'

I was sitting on the straw, leaning against the
wooden slats. Most people were sitting now. The noise
and motion combined to make me feel as though I was

being thrown along with the train in a net, dangling between the wheels. There was barely any suspension, insulation, separation between us and the track, the wheels, the ground. I would rather have been in a net, at least it would have let air through to us. The heat was stifling and the smell, well. It was like the steam from a pile of manure.

Aminah, the woman who had shouted at me in the camp and taken a blow from the Hungarian border guard, was squatting in front of me. I looked to my left. Dima.

'It's okay,' he said, 'she knows who you are. Nobody here is saying anything.'

'You fainted,' she said, 'I think you had a panic attack. I'm a doctor. I mean, I *was* a doctor.'

I felt ashamed, embarrassed. She was a doctor and the carriage was full of people who probably needed her attention more than I did. In fact I knew they did, because they'd all come from the camp.

'Thank you,' I said, struggling to look her in the eye. I realised how dry my mouth was.

'Where's my bag?' I asked Dima.

'Water?'

'Yes, please-'

'Make it last,' he said, handing me the bottle from the top of my bag.

'How long until the next stop?'

'It's about twelve hours until the stop in Romania,' Aminah said. 'I don't know if we'll be allowed off then, though. Or if we'll get anything to eat or drink.'

Dima shook his head. I took a mouthful of warm water and replaced the lid.

'I'm sorry if I was rude to you, when we first met,' she said, sitting down in the space between us and the next huddle of people.

'Oh, no, you weren't-'

'I was angry,' she continued, 'a few documentary crews had been round, the month before. Filmed it all. We thought something might come of it, but nothing did. Some of the charity workers really got to me, too. They were doing it to look good. You could tell. To have a story to tell their friends. Something to put on their next job application. A photo on their Instagram of them with perfect hair, giving out water to foreign kids. I was angry about all of it. Then you turned up and, well...'

'I'm sorry,' I said, thinking I could follow it up with something meaningful. Something to explain myself. I couldn't. I just repeated myself. 'I'm sorry.'

We sat without speaking for a while. I looked around at the faces I could see. Everyone was glistening. The air was thick. I wondered how much air was actually making its way through from outside and how much was just recirculating between us all. Some of us, like me, had big rucksacks that took up too much space. More, like Aminah, had practically nothing. Just the clothes they sat in. I felt guilty, just for the space my bag was taking up, let alone what was in it. We were all managing to keep the smallest margin of personal space. At that point, nobody was leaning against anyone they didn't know. It's amazing how quickly you lower your standards when you have to, though.

Eventually, people tried to sleep. Sitting back-to-back, leaning against each other, or against the wooden slats. The constant jostling and shunting of the carriage made it nearly impossible, though. You can't sleep when you're having to stop yourself from falling. I smelled something sour. Old milk, maybe. Blue cheese. It made me gag. I put my hand over my mouth and nose. It was too hot to stay like that, though. I felt like I would suffocate. I looked around to see where it was coming from. A girl, probably only a couple of years older than me, had been sick. Some of it was down her front, the rest was sliding down the wooden slats to her left, behind her. She must have turned her head to try to keep it away from everyone. I hoped it was just motion sickness, nothing more.

I tried to close my eyes and be somewhere else. I was being thrown around a boiling wooden box with a load of strangers who were desperately sad and sick, though, so I couldn't. It was stupid to even try. *This will end*, I kept telling myself. *It will end.*

I looked over at Dima. He had his eyes closed. *You're not sleeping*, I thought, *but I hope you're somewhere else.* I decided to try to use the time to plan out what to do once we got there. That was a stupid thing to try, just like sleep, and I knew it, but I had to have something to think about, otherwise I'd think about Jake.

***

By the time the train finally slowed to a stop, it was dark. It didn't make much difference. The daylight had only given us a gloaming through the slats, anyway. It was a relief, though, not to have to look people in the eye anymore.

I worked out it must be around midnight. I realised I'd missed my birthday.

'Don't you dare feel sorry for yourself,' I said, then stopped, looking up, realising I'd spoken out loud. I could tell Dima was watching me, although I couldn't make out the expression on his face in the dark. The train was still, for the first time since we set off. We were all listening, waiting for something, someone. The next stage. A thud on the wall shuddered through us all. There it was again. We looked in the direction of the sound, as though we could see through to the other side. The door rattled and finally light shot through as someone opened the door and shone a torch across us. I squinted. Aminah shielded her eyes. Dima looked straight ahead. I was sure I could see the track of a tear down his face.

'Up! Out!' the torch bearer shouted, then again in a few other languages. I struggled to find the straps of my bag in the dark. A hand caught mine. I looked up.

'I'm sorry,' whispered Dima, gripping my hand, 'forgive me.'

'What for?' I asked, feeling my guts tighten. *Shit. Has he told them who I am? Is this where I get carted off?* The bodies jostling past carried me with them, I stumbled and lost Dima's hand, turning to walk forwards.

It was even less of a station than the last place. There was nothing. Two guards with torches walked up and down the carriages, opening the doors and ordering everyone out. A few people from the other carriages ran to the grass verge and vomited. Others squatted or stood, letting whatever needed to come out spread over the grass. A guard stood, watching them, hand on his gun.

Nobody has come for me yet, I thought. *Maybe he meant he was sorry for getting me into this mess. He didn't, though, I did.*

I realised I was desperate for a wee. The nausea from the journey was in my bowels, now, too. I needed to do what they were doing. I couldn't. Not in front of Dima. But what if I didn't get a chance for another twelve hours? *I can't do that on the train.* I thought of the time I'd seen Aminah in the toilet area. *What's better? Doing it now or shitting yourself on the train? Fuck.* I was jigging.

'Are you okay?' Aminah said, putting her hand on my shoulder.

'I need the toilet,' I said, and realised my voice was cracking because I was starting to cry, 'not just a wee, either,' I laughed and sobbed at the same time. *Fuck's sake. Pull yourself together. Grow up and get on with it.*

'Sorry,' I said, wiping my eyes and sniffing, 'I don't know why I'm-'

'Don't worry,' she said, 'I'll help you. Come on. Bring your bag.'

I followed her as she walked over to the verge. The guard watched us.

'He'll be looking at you,' she said, quietly, 'there's nothing we can do about that. I can make sure no-one else is, though. Give me that,' she said, taking my bag and rummaging through. She dragged out my coat and put the rucksack on my left-hand side. She turned away from me and knelt down, directly in front, then held my coat out slightly behind her, to my right, so it formed the final part of my screen. She turned her head towards me, without looking.

'There,' she said, 'covered on three sides. There's nobody behind you. Get it done, quickly.'

I did. I scanned the crowd for Dima as I squatted down and was grateful that I couldn't see him. I was mortified that Aminah was so close, but I had no choice - it would have happened on the train if I'd tried to hold it in. I could feel the guard watching me and tried to erase him from my consciousness, as though I could just delete him like a bad photo. I grabbed a handful of leaves and grass as a makeshift wipe and pulled my trousers back up. I was so grateful to Aminah that I started crying again as I thanked her. She laughed.

'There are much, much worse things in life, believe me. You'll get used to it. Look, Dima doesn't care.'

I followed her eyeline to see him pissing up against a tree. *Come on,* I thought. *It's not the same.* I grappled through the contents of my bag to find my hand sanitiser and came across my watch. Hah. Five to midnight.

'If you'd have told me last year that my next birthday

would be spent shitting in a field in the middle of Romania, I'd-'

'HEY!' The guard shouted. I stopped and turned. It was Dima. He was running. The torchlight followed him, a shaking, pale shadow racing into the dark. It couldn't be right, but I swear I saw him fall before I heard the shot. Just a fraction before. I screamed and started to run towards him but Aminah grabbed me, held me back. There was shouting. Confusion. Two men started to run, some women shouted after them to stop. More shots. People falling, others shouting, screaming.

One of the guards fired his rifle up in the air. We all stood still, eyes moving between the guard and the bodies in the field. Some of them were moving. Dima wasn't.

The guards ordered us back on the train. I couldn't move.

'No,' I murmured, 'No-'

'You have to come now,' Aminah urged me, 'Emma!' she pulled my arm but I struggled away and ran towards Dima's body. She shouted after me. I felt a thud, a heavy smack to the side of my head. It threw me off balance. I stumbled, seeing sparks of light flash in the dark as I fell sideways, but someone hauled me up. It was the guard. He shouted something at me, but I couldn't hear. The world sounded as though I was under water, the rushing only pierced by a faint, high-pitched whistle. He dragged me back to the train. I couldn't focus. Everything in my eye line was sliding down to the bottom left of my vision, then back up to the right. I was trying to fight him, but my limbs wouldn't do what I wanted. He hauled me up to the open door and threw me inside, into the darkness. I fell to the floor. I could hear people around me, but all I could see was the square of moonlight, the doorway I'd just come through, swimming around in the darkness. I thought of the window of light behind the lorry driver. There was a hand on my arm, a voice in my ear, but I had only the dimmest sense of it. The door closed. We were in darkness again.

Chapter 10

I only remember patches. That girl who threw up, not long into the first journey - the one who tried to vomit into the corner to keep it away from everyone - it wasn't travel sickness. She was patient zero. Then we were all ill.

I think that's why I had to shit in the field, back at the first stop. And the others, vomiting as soon as they got out of the carriages. The whole train was ill, Aminah told me. I had a fever. We had matching bruises, on our left temples. Both from the butt of a guard's gun. Hers was fading. Mine was just reaching its darkest point.

'We're out of Bulgaria. We're in Turkey, now. I don't know how far down it is, though.'

That's the first thing I remember hearing her say. I was confused.

'We're in Romania,' I said, struggling to push my weight up off the floor. My top was soaked with sweat. My hair stuck to my neck and forehead. The smell. The smell was unreal. I knew we were all ill, before she told me. The smell could only mean we were all ill, and there was just this boiling wooden box, clattering along the tracks, for us all to be ill *in*. I blinked, looking around. Daylight. Tiny streaks of it, anyway, through the gaps in the wood. Glowing. The sun must have been fierce. It felt like we were under a grill. Lots of people were lying down, face-to-face, foot-to-foot, face-to-foot. Some curled up together. Some were leaning against the slats. Clammy. Weak. Grey. Not there, in their eyes.

'Emma? Are you back?' Aminah said, leaning over in my direction. Her eyes were amber. I hadn't noticed before. Like flames. I was staring at them.

'Emma?' she said again, searching my face.

'Sorry, yes. I'm here. You were saying we're in Turkey - but we're in Romania - we were in Romania-'

'I was talking to Zeyad,' she nodded her head in the direction of a man, quite old, maybe my grandad's age, lying on his side. Right next to me. I turned around and realised my head had been resting on the soft bend between his ribcage and his pelvis. *Fuck.* I'd been sleeping on his waist. Not sleeping. Sweating. Fevering. Fitting. Who knows. I could remember blurry pictures, frames, melting, mixing together. Nothing sharp.

'Shit, I'm sorry,' I said, 'I didn't mean to-'

'No, no,' he said, holding up his hand, 'don't worry. You kept me warm.'

He can't mean that. It's fucking roasting. Or maybe he's really, really ill. He looked frail. I didn't realise he could speak English. Until then, I hadn't heard anyone other than Aminah and Dima speak it. I looked around again.

'Where's Dima?'

'Listen, Emma,' Aminah said carefully, slowly, 'we're not in Romania. We're in Turkey. We'll be at the facility soon, I think. I don't know where Dima is. There's nothing we can do. You have to just focus on you, now. Hey,' she said, seeing my face crumple as I started to cry, 'hey. It's okay. When we get there, you tell them who you are, and you go home, okay? This has gone far enough.'

I put my face in my hands and sobbed. I knew she was right.

'It's okay,' she said, putting her hand on my back. 'You're going home, to your family. You were talking about them, a lot. Your mum, your dad, your brothers.'

Brothers. In my subconscious then, they were both alive. The thought just made me cry harder. I couldn't control the sobs. Everyone who wasn't lost in fever was watching me. I kept trying to catch my breath, to quieten down, but I couldn't hold it in. What Misha called 'ugly crying'. Snot. Red skin. Grimace. Saliva.

The voice that told me I was a terrible person started to hiss in my ear.

Selfish.

Cruel.

Dangerous.

Murderer.

Murderer.

You've killed him, it said. *Dima is dead because of you.*

I drew my legs up to my chest and hugged them, burying my face between my knees. *What have you done? What the hell have you done?* You *can go home.* They *can't.* He *can't.* I lifted my face.

'Do you know… do you know if he's alive?' I asked Aminah, trying to slow my breathing.

She hesitated. The train was slowing down. She looked at the door.

'Aminah, do you know?' I asked her again.

'No. I don't. I don't know if he's alive, but that doesn't mean he's dead. I'm sorry. I didn't see anything after you ran and the guard hit you. I was trying to stay with you...I never looked back.'

I nodded. 'Thank you.'

'She looked after you, you know?' Zeyad said. 'All this journey. You were very sick. She nursed you.'

A new wave of tears came over me. I nodded, tried to say thank you again, but only managed a strange sound.

'He's exaggerating,' she said, shaking her head, 'even

with the stop you were asleep for, it's not been long. I'm not sick, so of course I'm helping the people who are. You-'

We all lurched to one side as the train came to an abrupt stop.

You're going home, I said to myself. *You have to forget Anya. Forget Dima. Forget Aminah.*

The door opened for the last time. Binding white-hot sunlight and a wall of heat smacked me straight in the face. *How could it be hotter outside than in here?* We staggered to our feet, squinting. The sun was making my eyes water. I couldn't believe the heat, scorching the inside of my nose, my throat. It was like breathing fire.

I climbed out into the desert. That's what it felt like, to me, anyway. All I could see for miles was dry wasteland. Sand, rocks, scrub. In the distance, mountains, maybe. I couldn't see roads, cars, villages, anything. The sky was a cloudless, vast expanse of cornflower blue. The only thing to break it up was the white ball of fire we were all trying to shield ourselves from. The effort of holding my arms up to shield my face with my hands was too much, though. I let them drop. *You'll burn*, I said to myself, *you always do.*

Different guards, different uniforms. Same guns.

'Tell them,' said Aminah, 'go on.'

I stepped towards one of them, a man with a moustache and sweat dripping down his temples. I started to speak, but he shouted something I didn't understand and shoved me backwards. He carried on shouting, I'm not sure what the language was. This time he was shouting at everyone. People began to get in line. Aminah grabbed me, pulling me away from the guard, turning so he couldn't see our faces. We stood by the carriage.

'Your bag,' she said, 'do you have money? Get it out.

123

Hide it. Your passport, too - now!'

She squeezed my arm, pushing me down to the bag, in front of her so that the guard couldn't see. I squatted down and rifled through, shaking, fighting the urge to vomit. I found the envelope of cash and my passport and started to put them in the pocket of my jeans.

'No!' Aminah whispered, 'in your-' she gestured towards her crotch. I put the passport in the envelope, undid my jeans and stuffed it in my knickers. I fastened my jeans and as I looked up I caught my first glimpse of the facility. Between the carriages, on the other side of the train, there it was. I stood up. A prison in the desert. Aminah spun me round. The guard was making his way down the line, taking people's bags and throwing them a couple of feet behind him.

'Keep that where it is,' she whispered, 'at all times. Do you hear me? *All times.*'

I nodded. A man further up the line started to go through his bag, taking things out. The guard marched up and grabbed his arm, shoving him back in line, barking in his face. He picked up the things he'd retrieved and threw them into the dirt. The man was crying. I thought of my watch. *Shit. The photo of Jake and Benji. Did I bring it?* I couldn't even remember. I looked at my bag. Aminah caught me as I started to bend down.

'No!' she hissed, 'do you want to get shot?'

I straightened back up. *I didn't bring the picture*, I told myself, *I didn't. It's at home.* That watch was the only way I had of telling the time. *You have your bracelet, though. You have Anya looking out for you.* I held the threads around my wrist and took a deep breath.

The guard was moving closer. A woman was protesting about her bag. She held onto it. The guard shouted at her, pulling the straps. She held onto it and shook her head, saying something over and over. The guard's hat fell off as he tried to pull the bag away. She wouldn't let go, so he grabbed his gun instead, aiming it at her, shouting. The sweat on his head glistened, shimmering in the sun as his whole frame vibrated with his voice, screaming out. *Let go,* we all screamed at her, in our heads. *Let it go!*

She was crying, repeating the same thing. The guard gripped his gun, thrusting it towards her with each word he shouted. He made a final lunge for the bag and snatched it away, but she tried to wrestle it back. The shot made us all scream.

The woman lay on the floor, eyes open, staring up at the cornflower blue, blood seeping out from the back of her head through the sand. The bag was still in her arms. The guard bent down and snatched it anyway, throwing it behind him. He wiped the sweat from his face with his sleeve, out of breath. He shouted something at all of us, pointing to the gun that rested on his side, before bending down to pick up his hat. It was covered in dirt. He bashed it against his arm. I jerked backwards, startled at the sound, even though I could see it happening. A cloud of grey dust burst into the air and melted away. He put the hat back on. I let him take my bag. Everyone did.

***

I think of that woman, still.

What did she have in the bag? Was it something sentimental or something expensive? What if it was alive? I tell myself not to be ridiculous. Whatever it was, the threat of being shot wasn't enough to give it up. Did she know she would die, though? Shot in the head, at point blank range. Maybe she thought she'd get the butt of the gun to the temple, like Aminah and I did. She must have seen them shoot Dima, though. And the others.

My watch, my clothes, toiletries, utensils, tools - they were all gone. Mum's coat. The one Dima stole for me. I never found out what happened to them. Aminah was quiet. We were marched into a yard, just like the one on the video, with the chain-link fence. Except this time, when we were ordered to separate into men and women, nobody was behind the fence, filming. I wished they were.

There were a few adolescents with us, like me, but no young children. I guessed I was probably the youngest. There was a girl who spoke French who might have been around my age, too. She was travelling with her brother, I guessed, and their father. She stayed on our side, while they were moved to the male line. I wondered if this had happened to Anya. *Did she stand here, like this, waiting for the unknown? Wondering if she was going to be sent to a cell or to the wall?* My eyes kept going back there. A short section of the yard wall was dappled, like knots in tree bark, with random bullet holes. Red splashed across them, bled down from them, the trail tapering off before it reached the floor.

Why are you still not saying anything? I was too scared to try. It felt as though if someone coughed, they'd be shot.

What if we're all about to be shot anyway? I couldn't do it. Fear took hold of me. People talk about fight, flight or freeze. Well, I froze. I watched the same fear on the men's faces, a few feet in front of me. Zeyad swayed. The sun was fierce.

The guard stood between the lines and talked. *Does Aminah know what he's saying?* I couldn't read her face. She avoided my eyes. *She knows something I don't.* Maybe she knew what was going to happen. Finally, the guard gestured towards the archway at the end of the yard, shoving the first woman in our line in that direction and motioning for us to follow. *When you get there*, I told myself, *find someone and tell them.*

We shuffled under the arch, grateful for the shade. There was only one exit, to the right, which led us down a narrow stone passage. Every now and then a few missing bricks, blocked with iron bars, let light in. I looked around. A new guard. A woman. She was at the back of the line, counting us. *Tell her. Tell her when we stop.*

Light appeared, at the end of the passageway. The first woman stopped, then turned to look back at the guard. The guard motioned for her to go through, telling her to go, in French. *French.* I practiced what I would say to her as I followed the line outside. I was getting it all mixed up. The tenses, cases, conjugations. Simple nouns I'd memorised just this last year had gone. It had all evaporated from my brain in the boiling heat. She led us out, then stood back, lighting a cigarette.

White light hit me again. Another yard. Children. The space was full of children. *Here they are.* Chasing each other, squealing, doing handstands against the wall. The older ones kicking something between each other, like a football, but I couldn't make out what it was. The youngest was around five years old, maybe. Some of them looked older than me. The guard gestured to us, to walk around.

No Anya. There must be more here, surely. She'll be here, somewhere. Dima. Fuck, Dima! He was facing the other way, scratching into the wall with a stone. I looked around.

The guard had gone.

I shouted to Aminah, 'It's Dima!' and ran over to him. He turned, saw me, smiled. I stopped, not daring to hug him in case I hurt him. I looked at him, like he was a hologram. A ghost, an illustration. He was different. I scanned his body for a wound.

'Are you okay? Where did you get shot? Did they take you to hospital?'

'I wasn't shot.'

'What? But I saw-'

'I tripped. I heard them shouting after me, I started to run faster, then I tripped. I hit the floor and heard the shot, so I stayed there. Played dead. I thought they might leave me.'

'But - they shot the others, the ones who followed you - I think some of them-'

'Don't,' he said, shaking his head, 'I know.'

He fell back against the wall, then sank to the floor, his head in his hands. He was sobbing. *Shit. What have you done? Why did you say that?* I didn't mean what he thought. I meant, *I thought they would have shot you when they found you weren't dead, I'm so glad you're alive.* Not, *you led them to their death.* I sat next to him, put my arms around him. He leaned into me. We both smelled as bad as each other, so it didn't matter. I looked up at Aminah. She kept her distance, smiling sadly at us.

'I'm sorry,' he said, muffled by my t-shirt, 'I left you. I left because I was too scared. I knew where we were coming and...' he trailed off, crying into the space just under my collarbone. I stroked his hair, my fingers getting tangled in the curls.

How the fuck did this happen? The boy who was going to save you, who had all the answers. Did you think he was superhuman? He's a kid, just like you. He's scared. Alone. He has nothing. No-one. Like Anya. I shifted, the envelope crunkling between my legs, passport digging into my thighs on either side. *You can't leave Dima and Anya. It's your fault they're here.* At the time, I believed that. Dima came with me because I begged him to. That was clear. And Anya? If I hadn't gotten myself grounded, I could have got her out. I really did believe that, and it was slowly wearing me down.

'So you've been here before, then?' I asked, staring at

the football net that was chalked onto the wall. I imagined it riddled with bullet holes, streaks of blood, like in the other courtyard. Dima sniffed, sitting up. He nodded.

The guard came back. She looked relaxed. Strolling around the yard, smiling at the kids. The whole thing was surreal. Aminah watched her, then looked at me. I know what she wanted me to do. I shook my head, in a small, slow movement. She cast her eyes up and took a deep breath, watching the sky. I watched the children playing football and tried not to think about how much I missed Jake, or how much he might be missing me.

Chapter 11

We were kept in cells, except for when they made us work out in the courtyard. The girls were in cells with women. The boys under twelve were, too. The boys over twelve were kept together in their own cell. Dima, Mo, Asif and David. We were given a bucket of water, each morning, and shared a grey rag to wash ourselves with. I wanted soap, so badly. Shampoo. Toothpaste. Sun cream. Lip balm. I wished I'd Googled more things like that when I'd had a phone. *How do you make soap and toothpaste from…* well, nothing. I think maybe it was beyond Google.

I shared my cell with a woman who spoke French, so I tried to learn from her. Her name was Desange. She taught me some tricks. If you don't have toothpaste, or a toothbrush, but you have a piece of wood, it's better than nothing. You chew it, and it kind of works like chewing gum. She asked for the wire from my bra. I gave her the whole thing, because I didn't know how to extract it. It was damp and stained with the sweat of the entire journey. She didn't flinch at the smell.

Desange made my life better in there. I didn't tell her anything about who I was, where I was from. She never asked. I didn't ask for her story, either. We knew that neither of us wanted to talk about it. She used that bra wire to whittle away at the piece of wood to make us some toothpicks. At least we could pick out the bits of oat and potato from between our teeth, then.

In the morning, we got a bowl of grey sludge. It looked like snow does a few days after it's fallen, in spring, when most of it has melted away and all that's left is dirty slush at the side of the road, before it finally evaporates. I think it probably had the same nutritional value, too. Midday meal was always soup. It was served in a brown bowl and was so thin that it was hard to tell what colour it was. It smelled like a drain. We were too hungry to care. The last meal of the day was potato. Just potato. I looked forward to it, though, because it was familiar. It was filling. Nothing about it made me feel sick.

We rinsed our toothpicks out each morning. Sometimes, instead of having a wash, we would use the water to rinse out our clothes. Desange made a hanger from the wire, too, so we could let a couple of things drip-dry in the cell before we took them out into the sun when we had yard time.

I lost count of days. Was it days, or weeks? The journey there, the illness, the decision to leave and then to stay, the shock of seeing Dima again - I felt as though I'd been hollowed out. I was worn down by the guilt of leaving Jake, of what I'd done to Dima, of what I hadn't managed to do for Anya. I didn't give up, exactly, but I just sort of… stopped, for a while.

The daily grind of trying to keep clean, hydrated, fed - to try to get some sleep, to try to keep warm at night and cool in the day - it was enough. It sounds strange to say this, but part of me switched off. The constant adrenaline that had been fuelling me since I left to catch the coach to Dover, knowing it was only a matter of time until my head-start ran out and someone would come after me - then the knowledge that I was being chased, searched for, that I was on the run - that's what had kept me going.

Now I found myself way under the radar. Nobody could possibly know I was here. If any of those guards had been on the lookout for me, I'd have gone by now. If the staff in this facility were aware of the campaign to find me, or they'd been contacted by the UK, I wouldn't be an inmate still. As far as they were concerned, I was High Risk Worker #1407, kicked out of the UK for dangerous behaviour, and whatever my Russian-speaking country was hadn't decided what to do with me yet.

None of the staff ever tried to talk to me in Russian. I don't think they spoke it, or even cared where any of us were from, anyway. The other workers all knew I couldn't speak it, especially the ones from Eastern European countries. The odd occasion where I'd tried out my phrases gave me away. They didn't blow my cover, though. They all thought I was trying to find my sister. It got lost in translation, somewhere along the way, and I let them think it. God knows where they thought I came from, but they thought I was a Worker who had given up her clean record to search for her sister, so they loved me. I let them. Life was hard enough. If they wanted to think I was fearless and principled and driven by nothing but love, that helped me out.

The truth was much more complicated. I was scared. *Hypocritical. Selfish.* I began to question everything about who I was and why I was there. Had I come this far because I was desperate to find Anya, or was it because I was running away from home? Because I was just another teenager who was bored with the suburbs and wanted an adventure? Because I hated everything about growing up and being a girl and living online? Was that it? I didn't like thinking about it. I couldn't have done this to Jake, to my parents, for anything less than saving Anya. I told myself it was all for her. I could have done a million other things that were a lot less fucked up than this, if it weren't for her. Besides, I hadn't found her yet, and she had to be here. She had to be.

We got mixed up every day, during outside time. There were four different courtyards, that I'd seen, anyway. Each one had a different set of work to be done. It wasn't back-breaking labour, like Desange said the men had. It was peeling potatoes, washing plates, cutting cabbage, emptying and rinsing the toilet buckets. The children were expected to do the same work as the women. I couldn't figure out their system of who went where on what day. It seemed totally random.

Dima told me the best thing to do was to give it a while, maybe two weeks, and if nobody had seen a girl matching Anya's description in that time, she wasn't here. After maybe a week, I started to recognise most people. Every time I headed out into the sun, I would do two things: search for shade, search for Anya. Sometimes I found shade. I never found Anya.

***

'She's not here,' said Dima. We sat, the sun baking our backs, as we hacked away at the potatoes. I wasn't listening to him. Maybe I didn't want to hear him.

Why do they make us do this? Who gives a shit if the potatoes have skins on anyway? Isn't that where the vitamins and minerals are? Do they just want to give us something to do? Is this them being nice to us? Or is it to tire us out?

'Emma,' he said, 'she's not here.'

'I-'

My sentence was cut through by the sound of shots.

A few, within seconds of each other. Everyone looked over in the direction of the yard where the execution spot was. There were two brick walls between where we sat and the shots, but we all looked anyway, as though we could see the scene where the sound was coming from. I hadn't heard shots since we'd arrived.

'This isn't a game, Emma,' Dima said, 'you need to make a decision.'

I couldn't answer. I'd just heard bodies, falling to the floor. I was sure I had. *How many? What did they do?* About an hour before, the guards had come and taken a woman away. I didn't know if she was the mother of those children, the ones I was watching, but I was pretty sure she was. A boy and a girl, very close in age, or maybe twins. The girl was carrying a sack, following the boy as he walked between us all, picking up handfuls of potato peelings and throwing them in. The woman was always with them. She'd gone without a fight. *Was it because she didn't know what would happen, or because she did, and she didn't want them to realise?*

I felt tears rising, that familiar pressure behind the eyes, the rawness in the throat. There was no point trying to hold it back.

'What are they going to do?' I asked, as the first sob escaped. Dima followed my eyes. He stared at them too, then started to shake his head. He closed his eyes and put his head in his hands, covering his face. He had no answer.

'Hey,' said the guard, followed by something else in a language I didn't speak. We looked up at her. She was pointing at our pile of unpeeled potatoes, motioning for us to go faster. Dima picked up another and set to work.

I suddenly felt my adrenaline waking up again. I gripped the peeler. They were all clunky wooden ones, barely sharp enough to spread butter. It just added to the pointless activity - we must have hacked away half the potato with the peel by the time we'd finished. I wished it were a real knife. Even a metal peeler would do. Anything I could hurt them with.

'Emma!' Dima hissed, grabbing my arm, pulling me to face him. 'Stop staring at her, just get on with it! You want to end up like them?!' he gestured to the direction the shots had just come from. The guard looked back at us, every now and then, as she strolled around. I slowly picked up another potato. It was green, full of sprouting tendrils. *Go on.* I threw it. It hit her, right in the back of her head. She jerked forwards, then spun round.

Dima wrestled me to the floor. I dropped the armful of potatoes I was gathering. I don't know what came over me. I suddenly felt like we could take them down. If I shouted for everyone to help me, they would, and we'd stone them all to death. With fucking potatoes. I knew they had guns. I knew they used them. I'd lost my mind, I think. In that moment, I felt invincible. Convinced that this was all meant to happen and I was meant to start the fight back.

The guard marched over, blowing her whistle. Dima shouted in French: *She meant to hit* me, he said, *we were arguing, it was an accident.* Guards appeared at the entrance of the yard, hands on their guns. They ran over. We stood up. Dima shoved me behind him, putting himself between me and the guns. *It was an accident,* he repeated, *she threw it at me, I was insulting her family* -

The guard put her hand up and the guards behind her stopped, awaiting instruction. She said something, pointing to me, then Dima. They came for us.

Chapter 12

'You were right,' I said, looking at the chain between my wrists.

My back ached. At least we were together in a cell. Maybe because we were *children*. Maybe because they'd run out of space. I don't know. I still shudder, when I think of how things might have turned out if we'd not been in there together.

'I *was* right,' Dima said, looking at me for the first time since the yard. 'Do you know why?' he asked. I said nothing. 'I'm right because I know what happens, when you underestimate them. These people,' he gestured towards the door, 'the people who killed Anya's family, the ones that killed mine. Different groups. Different agendas. But they're all ruthless. More ruthless and brutal than you'd ever think possible.'

'They were killed?' I asked. It was a stupid question. What I meant was, *how*. Where. Why.

'All of them,' he said, staring at the wall ahead.

I stayed quiet.

'We were from the wrong group of people. A group of people they wanted to get rid of. When they took over our city, they got us first. Half of us were dead already, from the shelling. Some had managed to get out. To make the journey to Europe. My dad,' he stopped, looking down at his fingers. 'My dad said we couldn't leave my grandparents. They were too old, too ill to travel. He was stubborn. He was wrong,' Dima said, his voice breaking, 'he was wrong. We should have left them. But we always did whatever my dad said. Always. When he realised, he tried to get my mother and sisters out before they came for us, but it was too late. They were taken…'

He started to cry. His shoulders shook. His whole frame started to bounce with the sobs, making the chains between his wrists and ankles jingle. There was nothing I could say. He breathed slowly, deliberately, trying to carry on.

'My grandparents couldn't walk, so they shot them in bed. Then they took us – my brothers, my dad, me – to the place they were holding all the men and boys. We knew what would happen to us. We'd heard, from the other cities. I'd seen it on YouTube.'

I was crying as quietly as I could manage. It felt disrespectful, making a sound.

'I got away,' he said, 'because they thought they could sell me and my younger brother. Instead of slaughtering us. We escaped, from the back of the van. He didn't make it. I did.'

He stared at the wall again.

I couldn't begin to tell him how I felt, hearing it. I had dragged him back. Not to that place, but to somewhere close. Close in too many ways. I felt like the worst person. *You* are *the worst person.*

We were silent. I watched the tears falling down his face.

Sometimes, back at home, when I was upset, Jangles would stretch out her leg and put her paw on my hand, or my face, and hold it there, soft and silent. I shuffled closer to him and put my hands on Dima's arm. There was nothing else I could do.

We stayed like that for a long time.

I was the first one to speak.

'I'm sorry. I can't say anything more than I'm sorry… and I don't know how,' I paused, 'how to thank you…for what you said. What you did, in the yard. I can't explain it to you. I was just so angry. If people *knew* what this place really was, what they were doing, I swear-'

'They know,' he said, 'lots of people know. You think a place like this can exist, can take so many people from so many places and *process* them like they do, without a cooperation? Collusion?'

I opened my mouth to speak, but had no answer.

'The government know,' he continued, 'the police know. Security know. Civil Servants. The ones high up, anyway. They know. It's just a necessary evil, to them. We clean your offices, pick your fruit, build your houses…but if we step out of line, there's plenty more who will take our place. So you get rid of us. It's all legal. We come to a place like this, we wait to get reassigned to a less discerning country, with worse conditions. And if we really fuck up, you put us against a wall and shoot us. Or you make us Voids. You know what I did?' he asked, glaring at me, 'I was a Worker, on a building site in France. I saw the way they treated the North Koreans. Way worse than us. They practically starved them, I don't know how they managed to do any work. So I started asking questions. I had a phone. I recorded them, asked them questions, in secret, through the one who could speak English. I wanted to know why things were so much worse for them. But I never found out, because one of them reported me. I was arrested and they made me a Void, then sent me to Calais. I was just waiting to die, one way or another,' he paused, looking up at the grate at the top of the wall. A patch of sky, barred with iron. 'I was just waiting to die,' he repeated, 'when I met you,' he said, then shook his head, 'so like you said, what difference does it make?'

What could I say? Nothing. There's nothing I could say. It was my fault he was here. I thought of Anya. I had tried to get her to do exactly that. Film with a phone, gather evidence. I could have got her made into a Void.

'Anya's not here,' he said. 'I don't know what's going to happen to us. I think it might be time to tell them who you are. Unless you have a better idea.'

I shifted. We were sat with our backs against the brick, wrists and ankles shackled. My joints ached. My lower back was throbbing with knots of pain that stretched round to the front of my abdomen, down to below my belly button. *Shit.* I could feel it, coming down. I looked at the cell door. Listened. For now, there was no-one there.

'I'm sorry,' I said, 'I have to-'

I fumbled with the button and zip on my jeans. Dima started, then turned to face the other way.

'What are you doing?' he asked, watching the door. I reached into my pants and grabbed the envelope. There was just a couple of spots of blood on it. *Just in time.* I threw it on the floor in front of me and did my jeans back up. I was so embarrassed. You'd have thought I was beyond it, by then. No proper way to clean myself or my clothes, brush my teeth, wash my hair. Nobody else had, either. We all looked terrible, smelled terrible. Nobody cared. We'd lost so much dignity. But something about this was still excruciating.

Just a couple of weeks before, I'd kissed this boy who sat next to me now - and it felt like an out-of-body experience. If we'd been back home, I'd have agonised over how to do my hair, what to wear, whether my make-up was right, how many times to brush my teeth, even if I just thought there was a remote chance of seeing him. Now, here I was, weeks of dirt and sweat and grease all over me, sat right next to him. My breath must have been awful. His must have been, too. He was just as bad. We'd stopped smelling each other, I think. But this was different. He was a boy. I'd had that envelope between my legs, every day in whatever I was wearing, at all times, just like Aminah told me. Now I'd bled on it, too. I didn't think I was capable of being embarrassed or self-conscious anymore, but I was. I felt like I wanted to just disintegrate into tiny pieces and merge into the dirt under us and the bricks behind us. Dima probably smelled it before he saw it.

'What's that?' he asked, frowning.

I picked it up, in case the guard came in, and shoved it under my top.

'Shit, you can see it, can't you?' I asked, looking down.

He looked at the bulge and nodded. I could hear the paper crinkle, too.

'What is it? Were you hiding it all this time?' he asked.

'It's my passport, and my money. Aminah told me to get it out, before they took the bags.'

'How much money do you have?' he asked, sitting up. He started to glance at the door, then back at me.

'I don't know, erm… I think about £350, something like that - why? Can we get out of here?'

'Maybe. Let me do the talking.'

***

She's not here, I kept saying to myself, *she's not here. You saw everyone. Dima didn't find her. Aminah didn't find her. Desange didn't find her.* I felt awful, thinking about them. *I never got to say goodbye. Or thank you. What will happen to them?* I shook my head, trying to swat the thoughts away. £50. That's what our freedom cost. I should have paid for Aminah and Desange, too, but Dima said it was too risky. Besides, he said, we'd need the rest of the money to get out of Turkey.

After Dima found out about the money, he told me to ask the guard for help, for the bleeding. I couldn't, though, because I didn't know the language. I told Dima he would have to do it. The next time the guard came to look through the hatch in the door, Dima said something to him. The guard asked a question. Dima pointed at me, said something else. The bit of the guard's face I could see wrinkled up in disgust, frowning. He closed the hatch, muttering something.

'Well?' I asked, hearing his footsteps retreat.

'He's getting someone. It will be a female guard.'

Footsteps again. *Oh god. Please don't be the guard I hit. She hates me. She'll never help us. Never.* The hatch opened. Eyes appeared. They weren't hers. She said *here, it's all we have,* in French, and shoved some old rags through the hatch.

'Thank you,' I said, 'thank you-'

She closed the hatch.

'Wait!' Dima shouted. She opened it again. 'There's something else.'

That was all it took. The right person, the right amount of money. That night, once it was dark and she was back on duty, she took us out to the yard near the entrance. The one with the bullet holes. Part of me was convinced she was going to shoot us, for attempting to bribe her. I was trusting Dima with everything. He had the envelope. He kept it in the same place I did. He wasn't going to bleed all over it, at least. *Keep that where it is, at all times. Do you hear me? All times.* Aminah's words kept repeating in my head. I was trusting Dima with my life.

The guard told us to wait. She walked over to the front gate and spoke to the guards. Our wrists and ankles were still shackled. They looked over at us, then back at her. They lit cigarettes and wandered off, through the doorway we had just come through. They didn't even look at us as they passed. I watched Dima breathe in the smell of their smoke, deep, closing his eyes.

She beckoned us over. We shuffled across the courtyard, kicking up the grey dust as we went. She unlocked the gate. *This is happening. It's actually happening.* She caught my gaze. She spoke to me in French. *Be careful. You're vulnerable. Both of you. But you,* she pointed at me, *you especially.* I swallowed. She squatted down and undid the cuffs around our ankles. I watched her hair as she straightened up and took our wrists in her hands, fumbling with her keys. It was so black and smooth it shone like a mirror under the moonlight, glowing white. She clanked all the cuffs away onto her belt and opened the gate.

'Go,' she motioned, 'go, quickly!'

We ran.

We didn't know where we were running to. We just ran. I went left, instinctively. We were in the middle of nowhere, though, and there were no lights beyond the facility complex. We had no phone, no torch, nothing. We were running into the dark, into the cold. We just kept going. Every now and then we looked back at the facility, the lights retreating into the black. I expected alarms, sirens, flashing lights, dogs, guns. I ran as though there was. There was nothing, though. Nothing except the clear night's sky and a hundred miles of dirt. Rocks. Mountains on the horizon. Curving up at the edge of the earth, leaning back over us. I'd never felt so free in my life. I was bouncing, nearly falling headfirst with every stride, limbs flying, teeth rattling in my jaw.

'Emma,' Dima's voice panted from behind me, 'Emma, stop.'

I found it hard to slow down. I did it, clumsily, with heavy strides. I finally found myself tumbling over, rolling across the cold, sandy dirt, then coming to a stop on my back, facing up at the sky. It was beautiful. I was panting. Dima caught up and sat down next to me, then lay back too, stretching his arms out, breathing heavily.

We said nothing. Just stared up at the sky. Listened to our breathing. I'd never seen so many stars. It looked like the times I let Jake loose with the glitter and everything ended up saturated in the stuff. I smiled. The back of my left hand was touching Dima's right hand. I lifted it up and grabbed it, squeezing him tight. He squeezed back. We let them flop back down into the dirt, still together, but loose. Resting.

***

When I woke, dawn was breaking. Dima stood, scanning the horizon. I sat up.

'Where do we go now?' I asked.

He turned to look at me, holding out his hand. I got up and walked over to him, then took his hand. The air smelled so good. It smelled of so much more than I could see. We were in a barren wasteland, but with the slightest hint of damp from the night, evaporating in the first light of morning, I could smell trees, rivers, fires. I could smell the sea. The mineral tang of sea spray, for definite. I tasted my lips with my tongue. Salt.

'Is that sand, that tastes like salt?' I asked him.

He shook his head.

'It tastes like salt because it *is* salt. The sea is just over there,' he said, pointing a long ridge of rocks a couple of miles ahead. There was a blue line behind them that disappeared into the hillsides. A view of the ocean I'd mistaken for heat, shimmering off the rocks, changing the sky to a darker shade.

'That's where we're going,' he said, smiling, 'we should set off, before the sun gets too high. It's not far, but we don't have any water. Come on,' he started walking and called back to me, he grinned, 'you can decide what you want to do on the way.'

I ran to catch up. What was he suddenly so giddy about? This was like the Dima I first met. The one that charmed Julia, the one that teased Gerald. Cheeky. Light. The one I fell for. *Nearly. Nearly fell for.*

'What do you mean, decide?' I asked, realising how much my body ached from lying on the ground. My feet were blistered after running from imaginary bullets the night before, too. I was so thirsty. The water in the facility was dirty, but at least it was there. The only water I could see was two miles away, and I couldn't drink it. The salt on my lips just made the thirst worse.

'You have a decision,' he said, spinning round, talking to me and walking backwards. Almost bouncing.

'Hang on,' I interrupted, 'why are you so happy? Because we got out of the facility?'

'I'm going to New America,' he said, grinning, 'finally. Come with me, if you like,' he said, then turned and started running across the scrubland, towards the sea.

Chapter 13

The sun was higher in the sky by the time we reached the rocks. I'd forgotten about my thirst, my aching joints, my blisters, though. I had a decision. His voice repeated, in my head, as I watched him scramble across the rocks to the path, through the dunes.

'You can tell them who you are and go home, or you can come with me, to the only place where I can be free. The only place I've ever wanted to be.'

I think he saw my expression change. I looked doubtful. His face changed too, then. It became serious, intense.

'It's my only option, Emma, anywhere else and I'm dead. It's the only country who gives asylum to Voids.'

I nodded. 'I know they are, but-'

'They'll find Anya for you,' he interrupted, 'they're the only ones who will.'

He dropped it there, a grenade in my decision. He was making his way down the dune path. I watched him disappear. *Shit*. I'd been thinking about it for the last two miles. I knew what I should do. *I should go home*. But it wasn't what I wanted to do. Part of me did. A big part of me. I wanted to see Jake. I wanted to make sure I got back alive, for him, for Mum and Dad. But I had to find

Anya. Or find out what happened to her, at least. I didn't want to lose Dima, either. If I went back, whatever he did, I'd never see him again. If I went with him, though, and we made it - I could stay there. Get Mum and Dad to bring Jake. *We could all live there. Couldn't we? Why not?*

'Emma!' Dima shouted. He emerged back over the top of the rocks, motioning for me to catch up. I did. Behind him, the shoreline stretched away, up to a ragged headland. The sea was calm. Just half a mile inland, there was a town. Roads, cars, balconies, shop fronts. People.

Closer to us, just on the beach, men were hauling nets up out of the water. Silver, glistening bodies filled them. Writhing, straining to escape. The men undid the nets and the fish spilled out into waiting plastic crates. They slowed. Their frantic thrashing shrank to a listless bend here, a dull gasp there. I could see their gills, opening, closing. Slower and slower. Finally, they were still.

I stopped.

'I don't know what to do, Dima,' I said, standing at the top of the path. I wished Aminah was with us. I knew what she would tell me to do. I knew what everyone except Dima would tell me to do.

He sat down and sighed. I sat next to him, resting my elbows on my knees, looking out to sea, shielding my eyes from the sun.

'I don't want you to go home,' he said, 'but you should. You know you should.'

I looked at him. He was holding back tears. He cleared his throat, thumbed away a rogue teardrop, then sniffed, composing himself.

'That town,' he pointed to the life inland, 'is where the police station is. Head there. Ask for the police. Tell them who you are. Here,' he let out an awkward laugh and reached into his trousers to retrieve the package, 'take your passport and show it to them. You'll be home in a few days.'

I looked at the brown paper and the two firework bloodstains. I took it. The blood had soaked through to the top couple of notes in the bundle of cash, but the rest was unmarked. I counted the money. £300. This was supposed to take me to Berlin, with school. With all of them. I thought of Misha. She was my friend. So was Lisa. Did I miss them, though? *No.* I didn't. Did I want to go back to obsessing over my hair and my clothes and my likes? Back to trying to convince Misha that she doesn't need to start saving up for a boob job? Back to feeling stupid because Lisa will take the higher maths exam and I won't? Back to dreading PE every Friday afternoon when I have to run and sweat in front of Ben Kendall? *No.* I didn't. I didn't want any of that.

I took out my passport and looked at the photo page. *So young. That's not you, anymore.* I put it back in the envelope.

'What will you do?' I asked Dima.

He pointed to a cove, just in front of the headland. 'That's where the smugglers will be. They take people each night. Round to the harbour. Then they get them into shipping containers. That massive boat you can see, over there?' he pointed to a behemoth on the horizon. 'Like that. They're sailing to New America. Taking the stuff this continent still trades in with them.'

'How long will it take?' I watched the huge vessel imperceptibly shift. It never seemed to move and yet was definitely further away when I looked at it for a second time.

'About a month, I think.'

A month.

'Have you used the smugglers before?'

'No. I know people who have, though. To get to the

UK. Germany. I know people who have relatives that made it to New America.'

I took a deep breath.

'I'll be okay,' he said, 'don't worry about me. Give me your address. If I find Anya, I'll write to you.'

I started to laugh, then realised I wanted to cry, too. I tried to just cough, thumb and sniff it away like Dima did.

Anya. She was your friend. You've forgotten about her. If she's alive, she'll be broken. She'll need your help, to put the pieces back together, surely. She's been through everything you have and ten times more, without the safety of knowing she can always get back if she wanted to. Without a home or a family waiting for her. You could have saved her, but you gave up. She was your only real friend. The only one you actually looked forward to seeing. She listened to you. You loved listening to her. Her smile made you smile. Her laugh made you laugh. Did I miss her? Yes.

I'd been to Calais, I'd been to Turkey. The Worker Routes ended there. From that point, you're either sold to somewhere less discerning than the country that labelled you High Risk, or you're sent back to the place you fled in the first place, or you're killed.

Anya could be back in her home country, about to be bombed. She could be working in the depths of hell. She could be dead. It was impossible to get to her home country. If she was in the labour market in the places that accepted High Risk, there was no saving her. If she was dead, I would never know. But there was always that chance she was safe. That tiny chink of light through the crack in the wall. Maybe she got out. Maybe, with the right people around her, she could have done what Dima was about to do. She could have got on that ship to New America. She could be there right now. She got to the UK, didn't she? There was still the chance. After all this, could I just give up and walk away, when I knew there was one last door, left to open?

I handed the envelope back to Dima.

'You'd better hang onto this,' I said. 'I'll be bleeding for a few days, still. I'll have it back when it's safe.'

'What do you mean?' he asked, turning to face me.

'I mean, I'm coming with you.'

***

'Look - we can have a wash!' I cried, almost delirious at the prospect. We were in the town, walking around as though we had nothing to hide. *Surely the guards at the facility must live here?* I asked Dima when he told me where we were heading. He said not. It was a tourist town. They don't mix the two worlds.

In front of us there was a block of public toilets. Dima smiled.

'I'll meet you back out here in ten minutes, yeah?'

We split up, each going through our respective door on either side of the block.

Toilets. I hadn't seen a toilet since the portaloo in the Calais camp. I hadn't seen a real, porcelain one since I left our house that morning. I sat down and pulled my jeans and knickers down. *Fuck.* There was blood everywhere. The rags the guard gave me were saturated. It had seeped through to my jeans. Deep red. Wine red. The same colour as the blood that soaked the sand, behind her head. It made me see her again- the woman who was shot when she tried to keep her bag. Staring up at the sky. I closed my eyes and shook my head. *Don't. You can't do that now.*

I took a deep breath and pulled as much toilet roll out from the holder as I could carry. I waited. There was one other woman using the toilets, in the cubicle next to me. I waited for her to flush, open the door, wash her hands and *tak-tak* her flip-flops over the tiles, out of the door. I came out of my cubicle and saw soap. There was soap. To the side of the sinks there was a stool, in front of something that looked like a bidet, maybe, but without a basin - just a tap jutting out from the wall, above a grid to drain away the water. I sat on the stool and took off my shoes and socks. The socks pulled some skin away with them, from blisters that hadn't healed. I winced.

'Fuck!' I said under my breath, turning the tap on. I said it again when the water hit my feet. It was so cold. The wounds stung like hell, but I knew that was a good thing. I tried to get as much of myself clean as I could, between the sink and the wall tap, with the soap. I even had a go at washing my hair. I hadn't had access to soap for so long. I washed my mouth out with it, just like my nana used to say she would, when I swore.

Finally, I emerged into the sun outside.

'What took you so long?' Dima asked, looking up at me from his perch on the low wall.

'I washed my hair,' I said, squeezing the water out of the ends. The splashes on concrete reminded me of holidays. Wringing out my hair by the side of a swimming pool, in the sun. The whole place reminded me of holiday. It didn't sit right. It made the past few weeks seem like a bad dream. Bars. Cafés. Shops selling sunglasses, souvenirs, sarongs. People in flip-flops, sauntering along, laughing, licking ice creams. Kids, just like Jake. Just like the ones that had lost their mum in the facility. These kids had their parents with them, though, and they weren't collecting everyone's potato peelings into a rubbish bag. They were playing with the water in the fountains, mithering their parents to buy plastic toys and hair braiding from the roadside sellers.

'We need to get things from the market,' said Dima. 'Everyone else will have stuff with them. We don't.'

'Can we afford it?'

He nodded.

'We're not paying. Come on.'

There was a market, in the town square. *Clothes. I need clothes.* I was relatively clean, finally, but my clothes were disgusting. I hated pulling them back on over my washed skin. It forced me to acknowledge how far I'd gone, without realising.

I'd never stolen anything before. I watched Dima. He made his way through the stalls, picking up this and that, totally unnoticed. *How is he doing that?* He just walked between them all, like he was walking through his house, picking up laundry. He even stopped to talk to some of the stall owners. He could speak Turkish. Of course he could.

All I wanted was some clothes. I wandered up to a stall selling hareem pants and t-shirts.

'Hello,' the stall owner immediately addressed me, in English.

'Hi,' I said, feeling the fabric of one of the pairs of trousers, trying to look casual.

'Can I help you?' she asked.

Shit. I can't do this.

'Just browsing, thanks,' I saw Dima appear behind her, smirking at me.

'Are you okay?' she asked, looking at the blood all over my jeans, the dirt all over my T-shirt.

'I'm fine,' I faltered, 'I… fell down.'

Dima wandered away, quietly laughing.

Fuck off, I thought. But I wanted to laugh, too.

'Oh no, are you okay?' she asked, putting her hand on my shoulder.

'I'm fine,' I repeated, 'thank you.'

I walked away. *It's not going to happen.*

I sat in the shade of a tree, on a low wall at the edge

of the market. I could hear running water. It was the sound of a drinking fountain, just a few feet away. I got up and drank, wishing I had bottles to fill. When I turned back around, Dima was sitting in my place. He smiled at me. I thought of how absurd the whole situation was. It felt like we were on holiday. Brother and sister, cousins, family friends, whatever. As though we'd just popped down to the town square, to pick up some bits and bobs to take to the beach for lunch. Boyfriend and girlfriend, looking for souvenirs from our first holiday together, playing house in the apartment. *Which would we be?* I smiled, thinking of our kiss all that time ago. Watching him look up at me now, the rest of the world was muted.

He was in focus, everything else was blurred. Dimmed, quiet. Just Dima, and his green eyes, smiling back at me. He looked down.

'Come on,' he said, holding up a bag, 'I've got something for you.'

I followed him as he walked out of the square, back to where the toilets were. He reached into the bag.

'Here,' he said, 'I don't know if they'll fit, but…'

He handed me some folded clothes.

'I'm going to get changed,' he said, 'I'll see you out here, yeah?'

He walked into the men's. I looked down at the fabric in my hands. It was the T-shirt I wanted from the stall. Some trousers, too. Hareem pants. I unfolded the last item, a hooded zip-up top, and something fell on the floor. A packet of sanitary towels. I laughed.

Dima, I think I love you.

I let myself think the words, and feel them, too, just for a minute.

***

It looked like a postcard. A deep orange sun, a pink haze and a violet sky. The sea, pearl-grey-blue and gently rippling. The sand along the shoreline, losing all the footprints from the day with each lap of the water. The cliffs, rocks, ancient and rested.

If we weren't about to risk our lives in the hands of the strangers who were standing over us with guns, it would have felt like a honeymoon.

'You can still go to the police station,' whispered Dima, 'it's not too late.'

'If it's not too late, why are you whispering?' I asked. 'Why do they have guns?'

We were in the cove, out of sight of the town, with a group of others who wanted to make the crossing. We all sat on the sand together, as though we were about to have a picnic. Four men, dressed in khaki and black, stood between us and the route back around the cliffs to the beach.

'The guns aren't for us,' Dima said, 'it's just protection. In case the police show up.'

'Great,' I said, 'that makes me feel much better.'

'I mean it,' he said, putting his hand on my arm, 'like I said before - it's dangerous. *Really* dangerous. I don't know what's going to happen. People die.'

He *did* tell me that.

I was so angry with him, for a long time, but looking back I have to acknowledge that. He did warn me. While we were walking through the wasteland, he told me the horror stories. I knew people died, before he told me. My social media timelines were full of it. Sometimes the news channels covered it. We'd all seen the pictures. That one photo, especially. It's amazing, what you can ignore, though, when you really want to.

I ran through the evidence again, to give it another chance to change my mind. Dima had nearly been killed once already. The men who followed him were dead or injured. The woman who held onto her bag was dead. The one with two kids in the facility was dead. Who knows what might have happened to us at the facility if we'd stayed there? We could've been next. This would be the most dangerous step of the journey so far, undoubtedly.

The voice of my rational brain was screaming at me to walk to that police station. I was slowly being dragged over the edge of a sheer drop into darkness. Trying to decide whether to shout for help, or jump in.

You don't want to die wondering! I could hear granddad's voice say. He would always say that, whenever I was scared to do something. When I asked him what he meant, he said: *It means, you don't want to be on your death-bed, regretting the things you didn't have the nerve to try, the places you were scared to visit, the people you didn't tell how you felt about them. You don't want to be wondering what could've been, if only you had been brave enough. Don't end up like me,* he said.

I'd come this far. Was another month going to make the difference between my family being okay or not? *No. No it won't. The camp will have told them I was fine, when I left. They know I've got something to do, and I'll be back when I've done it.* I didn't believe what I was saying to myself, but I still needed to tell myself the lies. *As soon as we get to New America, I will call them. Anya needs me. Dima needs me.*

'I'm coming with you,' I said, 'for Anya. For you. For me.'

Dima smiled. I could tell he was relieved. I think he knew he should be persuading me to go home, but he wanted me to stay. I remembered that feeling. I was so desperate to get him to come with me, when we left the camp. I needed him, for my safety and my sanity. I practically begged him. There's no way I could have done it without him. Now, here we were, on the final leg of the journey I had started, the journey I had been hell-bent on taking and so *insistent* that he come with me for.

Of course I couldn't make him finish it alone.

Besides - I set out to find Anya and she was still out there, somewhere.

The men shouted at us, waving us over. We all got up, eyeing a small boat that was bobbing up and down in the surf behind them. I started to breathe in through my nose and out through my mouth. It was a reflex I'd developed whenever I started panicking. It never helped.

The tiny sliver of sun above the horizon was sinking. I watched it disappear completely as we stood, feet wet in the foam, waiting for further instruction. One of the men waded through the surf and climbed up into the boat, shouting at the man on the shore, who untied the rope that was mooring it to a post in the sand. All the men shouted at us, as the boat began to drift. The ones left on the land shoved us forwards, then dragged us into the water. One of them got into the boat, while the others hauled people in. Now that the sun had gone completely, the water was black. Black and cold. It took my breath away. I couldn't have screamed if I'd wanted to. I kept putting one foot in front of the other, terrified of the unknown all around my legs and under my feet, until I was lifted up and dragged on board. I scrambled over into a corner and sat with my back against the wood, watching the others follow. Dima was climbing in. Water dripped off his trousers and trainers, pooling on the wooden planks underneath.

There were about twenty of us, mostly young men, around Dima's age and a few years older. There was only a handful of women. Four, five if you included me. I was the youngest. The man near the engine started it up. The boat shuddered. I watched the ripples stretch away, lit by the glow from the rising moon, as we ploughed into the darkness.

I felt caffeinated, as though the sea breeze was full of amphetamines. I breathed it in, imagining my lungs coating with crystal powder. Something to counteract the heaving bile in my stomach. My hands were shaking. I realised one eyelid was twitching. Fight, flight or freeze. My body wanted to fly. To stand up and throw myself over the side, take my chances in the icy abyss to swim back to shore and the police station. *They'd shoot you in the water. You know their faces. You know what they're doing. They wouldn't let you get away.*

I watched the shore disappear behind the rocks as we skimmed around the headland. There was the harbour, up ahead. Floodlit, like a football stadium. The size of the ships caught me off guard. With the light behind them they looked like mountains. Like hulking sections of the mainland, that had been cut off and set adrift. It gave me vertigo, just looking at them. I felt sick. Watching the sea instead didn't help. We were bashing up and off the waves now, buffeting up and down.

Concentrate. I looked at Dima. His eyes were fixed on the shipping containers - metal crates that could have been freight carriages, in red, orange, green, blue. They were stacked like house bricks, forming a wall, rising up from the deck of the biggest ship - the one that looked like the whole coast had come loose. A crane was slowly manoeuvring a brown, weather-beaten container into an empty corner. I watched Dima watch them, knowing he couldn't wait to be in one of those rusty boxes.

How will we breathe?

Our boat slowed as we drew nearer to land. We were pulling into a small bay just next to the harbour, hidden from it by a shoulder of rock. I could see steps, leading from the beach up to the road that led to the harbour. A truck was waiting, with a container on the back. Dima saw it. He swallowed. My body suddenly jerked forwards and I had to make an effort to lean over the side of the boat. I spewed bile into the sea.

I fell back, watching Dima. He didn't look at me. The engine spluttered out. We floated in silence for a second before the men stood up. They climbed over. The black water came up to their knees. Two made their way to the shore. The others stayed, shouting at us. Dima gripped our bag and finally looked me in the eye.

'It will be okay,' he whispered to me.

I watched him climb over and followed. The water took my breath again. I felt like a tiny creature, something you could only see under a microscope. The ships, the rocks, the truck, the men. They were huge. I was lost in the waves, thrown all over, batted between them all. Our cat Jangles used to bring in mice, sometimes. Terrified, tiny mice. She tortured them to death. Batted them between her paws, tossed them up in the air, let them run off, only to catch them by the tail and drag them back to her. They kept trying, kept going, their black eyes glinting to the last. Eventually something would kill them.

Exhaustion, fear, a broken neck. She would keep playing with them, long after they died. Right now, I felt like one of her mice when it was fighting to stay alive. I couldn't shake the feeling that this would end the same way.

Chapter 14

We sat on the beach, waiting. We were supposed to stay there until we were told to move. Two of the men returned to the boat and started the engine. They shouted back to the men left on the beach, pointing up to the top of the cliff face behind us. We looked up. More men. Wearing balaclavas, this time. I turned back to see the boat speed off into the ink.

One of the men shouted something and the people around us started to get up, so we did the same. He grabbed a couple of people, pushing them in the direction of the steps. Both women. A young man, Dima's age, followed, but he was pushed back.

'No,' the man said, the first words of English I'd heard him speak. 'Women only.'

I wanted to vomit again. Dima's eyes widened. He looked at me. His eyes said *run*. I couldn't. It was too late. I was being dragged by my arm. Dima stepped towards us. I saw him stop as the man dragging me pointed a gun at him. He halted, holding his hands up.

The man let go of my arm and shoved me up onto the first step. I did as I was told. I walked up the stone stairs with the other women, too scared to look back at Dima. I couldn't make the steps out in the gloom and stumbled a couple of times. The man grabbed my arm, pushing me forwards. I watched the women in front of me as we emerged into the light, cast from the docks. We were still out of view to all, except the floodlights.

The first woman was wearing red jumper and stonewash jeans. Another was in a black hijab and abaya. The third was in a grey coat, like the one Dima stole for me, and black trousers. The fourth was wearing a long skirt, top and headscarf, all made from the same green and orange patterned fabric. I don't know why I concentrated on their clothes. I think it was because I didn't dare look them in the eye. I didn't want to see the expression on their faces. To see their eyes, glinting, just like mine, just like the mice.

The truck loomed up on our left-hand side. I let myself glance down at the beach. Dima and the others were there, one man pacing in front of them, pointing his gun idly in their direction.

'Hey!' the man behind me shouted and pushed me onto the road. Men with balaclavas stood at the back of the container. It was red on the outside, with white letters. I couldn't read the word. They called us round to the back. We finally looked at each other as we walked over. Their eyes looked just like I knew mine did.

There was no throwing a vase at a TV this time. No escape through the bedroom window. No hitting someone over the head with a gas canister. There was no bribing guards to be done here. We knew what was going to happen, and we knew there was nothing we could do to stop it. They swung the doors open and ordered us to get in.

There were no lights in the container. We walked past the guns, past the hidden faces, up into the darkness. I took a deep breath. All I could hope for was not to die. *Just survive*, I told myself. *You have to survive this.*

I couldn't see the back of the container. It was too

dark, like looking into a cave that carried on down into the ground for miles. I could hear our fear. We were shaking, panting. One of us was crying. I couldn't tell you if it was me, or someone else. I just remember hearing it. Soft, slow. I still hear it, sometimes.

I turned to see the window of light and the road outside, obscured as the men climbed up. They took off their balaclavas. I remember thinking, *why?*

I felt them, the women next to me, being knocked down like bowling pins. Then I went down, too. I hit the back of my head on the metal floor. I wish it had knocked me out. One of us screamed. I looked to my left. The woman in the patterned outfit was lying next to me. I don't know if it was moonlight or the floodlight from the docks, but something lit her up. The colours in her outfit glowed. Shimmered. My knees caught my eye, the hareem pants almost exactly the same colour as the sky. There was a shadow in front of me, bearing down on me. I looked to my side again and focussed on her face. I could see tears, running from the outer corner of her eye, down to her ear. She looked at me and I felt something, a hand, grasping mine. We gripped each other while the shadows loomed. She squeezed my fingers as it began. I felt cold around my pelvis and felt my own tears fall, too.

I became aware that the shadow above me was saying something. A harsh, gunfire phrase that I didn't understand. I was being dragged up. The shadow became a man, shouting and gesturing at my legs. The blood looked black in the moonlight. He'd pulled down my knickers and seen blood. It ran down my legs as I stood there, staring at it. He spat at me and yanked my pants up, throwing me out of the back of the container. I fell, heavy on the tarmac, winded. I rolled over, clutching my ribs, and looked out across the sea.

I tried to get up, but my ribs felt like they were on

fire. I lay back down and looked up at the sky. I could hear them, in the container. I still hear it. I could see clouds, racing over the moon. I heard footsteps. I didn't want to see whoever it was. I didn't want to look at another human being. I stayed there, staring at the grey wool, dragging over the moon.

'Emma!'

The voice sounded as though I was listening to it from underwater. I didn't move.

'Emma!' clearer, louder this time.

I turned my head. Dima. He was standing with the other men. Their wrists were bound. He was crying. I watched his tears and felt nothing. I looked back up at the sky.

***

Here I was again. On the back of a truck, in the dark, waiting to be cast adrift.

We were all together now. The clothes adjusted, the sweat dried, the pulse slowed. Someone had a torch.

Somehow, the bags had made it with us. Maybe they knew we'd die without them, and if nobody survived the journey, how would they tell their families back home that it was possible to make it over there? That's the logic I clung to. The thought that helped me to believe that some of us *would* survive.

Being lifted onto the ship felt incongruously like a ride at a theme park. I'd lost all sense of danger. Nothing seemed to phase me, now. None of us women were scared about the physical danger anymore. The men flinched at every jolt and sway. They looked around, as though they were straining to see what was happening. We didn't. We just breathed and waited for it to pass.

I imagined us rolling around the inside of a drum. A

wall of death. Those fairground attractions where you watch a man on a motorbike circle the walls as though he's defying gravity. I saw us being shaken up in the box like dice in a fist, blank faces and limbs everywhere, like puppets with their strings cut.

We landed with a hard crash that sent me bowling over to my left-hand side, into the arms of the woman in the black abaya. I wanted to stay there, in her lap. Curl up, bury my face in her stomach, close my eyes and forget.

I apologised and sat up. Dima caught my eye. All I could see of him was a spectre. Just cheekbones and eye sockets in the torchlight. I knew what he was thinking. *She hates me.* I did. I closed my eyes. I wouldn't sleep, but I would pretend to sleep, for as long as I could.

Within the hour, I think, we were sailing. I could tell. The light changed. The sounds were different. The temperature changed. That's how we measured the passage of time, too. Light, sound, temperature. One corner of the container was designated as the toilet. I just didn't care about any of that anymore. We tried to ration food and water. Dima and I shared what we had in the bag. Some of us had more, some had less. It didn't matter. After a week or so, everyone was running low. On water, especially.

You'd think, maybe, that you'd just get used to it. I got used to the hunger, to an extent. Stopped feeling it, to a point. But the thirst was different. When your lips are flaking, your pee is burning, your mouth is itching because it's so dry, you can't just ignore it.

'How do they expect any of us to survive?' one of the boys said. He was the same age as Dima, maybe a bit older. His words cut through the fog between us all, one day when we were feeling the airless heat even more than usual.

We looked at him. I didn't know he could speak English until then. Everyone was listening.

'There's no air. No water,' he said, wiping the sweat from his forehead, shaking his head.

'There's enough,' the man opposite him interrupted, 'enough for us to do this. It's enough.'

'Are you mad? We're dying in this box. You know we are,' the boy said, his voice hoarse.

'No,' the man answered, sitting up, 'we were dying *where we were*. We're being reborn, here. You'll see. This is like the journey down the birth canal, out of a different womb, into a better world. Remember the statue. Her poem. Haven't you seen it?'

The boy frowned. We all watched.

'Seen what?' he asked.

'The statue waiting for us.'

The man scanned our blank expressions.

'The Statue of Liberty is the symbol of *New America*,' he said. 'She will make sure we get there. She will greet us, when we do.'

The boy rolled his eyes, shaking his head.

'No,' the man said, 'don't do that. She will. You know what is written on her?'

That's when he quoted the poem. He spoke the entire thing, almost sung it, word for word, with so much feeling. We all watched his eyes, his mouth, his teeth, his hands, beat out every word like they were his heart:

> *Not like the brazen giant of Greek fame,*
> *With conquering limbs astride from land to land;*
> *Here at our sea-washed, sunset gates shall stand*
> *A mighty woman with a torch, whose flame*
> *Is the imprisoned lightning, and her name*
> *Mother of exiles. From her beacon-hand*
> *Glows world-wide welcome; her mild eyes command*

163

The air-bridged harbor that twin cities frame.

'Keep, ancient lands, your storied pomp!' cries she
With silent lips. 'Give me your tired, your poor,
Your huddled masses yearning to breathe free,
The wretched refuse of your teeming shore.
Send these, the homeless, tempest-tost to me,
I lift my lamp beside the golden door!'

I realised tears were running down my face.

...Give me your tired, your poor,
Your huddled masses yearning to breathe free,
The wretched refuse of your teeming shore.
Send these, the homeless, tempest-tost to me...

The words still hurt me. They make me feel everything
I'm lacking. I've tried, again and again, to do something
to help. I always come up short. I always will.

Anya was one of the *tempest-tost* before she even
came to Lulworth. Most of her family had been killed. As
far as she knew, the survivors were in the Worker
Scheme too, but she had no idea where. She came on a
boat, too. From Libya to Greece. It was the most
common way to get from Africa to Europe. It was just a
rubber dinghy, though. So much worse than what I was
going through. I couldn't imagine it. To me, being stuck
in the container felt like the worst thing anyone could
endure - but at least we had shelter from the wind, rain,
the cold, the sunlight. We weren't going to be capsized
and drowned. We were in a medieval dungeon, stacked
high on a brutal stack in the ocean - but at least it was
secure. *Tempest-tost*, maybe, but only in our minds, at least.

More days and nights passed. I kept thinking that the
man who spoke up was right. Surely, they couldn't think

we would survive it. Not really. The food was gone. We had some water, still. Only a little. I hadn't spoken a word to Dima since dry land. I could look him in the eye when I really had to. Nod. Shake my head. That was it. We shared what was in the bag. I knew the constant burn, not just when I peed but *always*, wasn't right. Nobody wanted to use the toilet corner. Not out of embarrassment. We were past that. It involved getting up and walking, though, and we didn't have the energy. It made me dizzy. Faint. My head would swim. Stars would spark up in my vision. I fell to the floor a couple of times. I wasn't bleeding any more, though. That was something.

I tried to pass the time by listening to the sounds outside the container and imagining the worlds they came from. Setting up stories in the scene that came to mind. I closed my eyes and listened to the creaking hull. The sound started deep under the surface of the water, in the very bottom of the belly of the boat. From underneath, I could see that the ship was bigger than anyone could comprehend, you couldn't see it all at once, no matter how far away.

Imagine you're swimming next to a sheer cliff face, under the water, and you're watching the rock in front of you, above you, below you. It goes on forever. Suddenly it moves. The whole mass moves and begins to travel alongside you. Imagine how overwhelmed you'd feel. How vulnerable. That's how I felt, under the hull in my mind.

What was inside the base of the ship? I saw a labyrinth of corridors, networks of pipes, machines in perpetual motion. Were there people down there, too? Working below the surface? Or were there others like us, stowaways, trapped like mice in a maze? This place was dark. I decided to leave.

165

I opened my eyes and watched Dima. He was asleep. Or just somewhere else, like me. His patchy facial hair had grown thicker since we left Calais. He looked older. The darkness under his eyes seemed to be spreading wider and wider, like shadows creeping across sand. I wondered what I looked like. I couldn't remember the last time I'd seen myself in a mirror. I felt my face with my fingertips. *Filthy.* Rough with dirt, sweat, dehydration. It felt like there was less of me. My skin was too tight over my bones. *Close your eyes.*

I listened. Filtering out all of our rasping breathing, our coughing and creaking, I could hear the sea. The wind. Sometimes I thought I could hear birds, but I didn't dare think it was true. That would mean we were near land. I told myself it was the wind, whistling through the metal maze. The sea. *Think of something good about the sea.* I took myself back to holidays at the beach, as a kid. The smell of sun cream, the taste of salt, the sound of feet splashing in and out of the surf. The satisfaction of tipping out a bucket of sand that stayed tightly packed and perfectly castle-shaped when you revealed the contents. I smiled. *Stay here.* I never could, though. The beach became the one I watched Dima and the other men on, looking up at us through the dark, before we were ordered onto the truck. The smell of sun cream became the smell of the lorry driver's breath. The taste of salt became the taste of the sulphurous soup at the facility. The sound of splashing became the sound of shots being fired. The feeling of gripping the sand bucket became the feeling of squeezing her hand as she lay next to me.

At the time, I didn't realise what this all meant. I just knew that something had changed in my brain, and I didn't know if I could ever change it back.

One night, in the torchlight, I watched her. The

woman in green and orange. The one who I held hands with, that night. She wasn't well. She would breathe fitfully, sweat beading on her brow, eyes closed, shuddering now and then, clutching her clothes around her.

'She's ill,' I said, to everyone, as though they could do something about it. The people who understood me looked at her. She didn't open her eyes.

What could we do?

The next morning, she looked grey. I hauled myself up, seeing stars again, steadying myself against the corrugated metal as I made my way down the container to her. The only sound she made was her shallow, rasping breaths. Her eyes were open, but I didn't think she could see me, or see anything, beyond the visions of her fever-dream. She was curled on her side, in the foetal position, staring straight ahead.

'She's really ill. She needs a doctor,' I said, looking at each passenger in turn.

Eyes stared back at me.

'Does anyone know her name?' I asked.

A few heads shook. More blank faces.

Green and orange flashes caught my eye and I looked down at her again. She was fitting. Her limbs, neck, chest all jerked and her breathing sounded wet, saturated, as though her throat was filling.

'She's dying!' I shouted, 'We have to get help!' I started banging on the corrugated iron, shouting. 'Help! Help us, there's someone in here dying, she's going to die!' I screamed up at the grates. Nothing. I grasped at the doors, trying to prize them apart where they met in the middle, but it was pointless. They were sealed and locked from the outside. I banged on the doors again, shouting, screaming for someone to help. My fist drew back sharply. Someone was holding my wrist back. I turned. It was Dima.

'She's dead,' he said, gripping my arm.

'What?' I asked, looking down. She was completely still. Silent. Eyes open.

'She's dead,' he said, quietly, 'and nobody is coming. Nobody can hear you. You need to sit, down, save your-'

'Don't speak to me,' I said, snatching my arm away. I knelt down next to her. Her breathing had stopped. I held her wrist. He was right. No pulse. I placed her hand by her side and felt the hooded top tied around my waist. I undid its arms and brought it to my front, then spread it out over her like a blanket, drawing it up over her head to cover her face.

The container was silent. Back in my place, I closed my eyes and tried to go somewhere else.

Chapter 15

One morning I was sitting, counting the stitches on my waistband again, when we all turned towards the direction of a sound outside. We hadn't heard anything other than the weather, the sea and the ship for so long. It wasn't any of those. It was the sound of voices. Distant, but they were voices. There was another sound, too, a mechanical sound. Not under us in the ship, though. Outside. It sounded like it was in front of us.

Chains. An engine. A different engine.

We sat up. Straightened our backs. Nobody said anything. We just listened.

'Hey!' I heard one of the voices outside shout. I heard something ending in *down here*, too, but couldn't make the rest of it out. They were speaking in English. With American accents. I was sure of it. The man who quoted the poem on the statue smiled. He broke into laughter. Tears began to fall from his eyes.

'We're here,' he said, 'we're here!'

The woman in the abaya replied to him in another language. She held her face in her hands, crying, smiling at him. I don't think the rest of us dared to believe it. We looked at each other, still silent.

Every now and then someone would look at her. Lily, I named her. The woman in the corner, who had been dead for days, covered in my hoodie. I named her Lily, because her outfit reminded me of my mum's favourite flowers. Tiger Lilies? Whatever the orange ones were. Flame orange flowers and vibrant green leaves.

Every now and then I would look at her, too, and that's why I didn't dare to believe it could soon be over. I felt guilty. I felt as though, if we were all about to walk out of there, then she was the cost of the journey. Her body would be left here, because her life was the price paid for our passage to the free world. I didn't just feel it. I knew it.

A loud clang against the roof made us all jump. The noise of the engine grew louder, joined by a high-pitched whirring. I felt a rush of blood away from my gut and into my limbs. Fight, flight or freeze. I was ready to run. But where could I go? The adrenaline was useless.

Then it began. We were lifted. We rocked to one side, then the other. The motion levelled out, settling into a gentle sway. The whirring was drowned out. Everyone was talking, shuffling, putting things in bags, getting their shoes and coats on. As though we were just coming to the end of a long coach journey and we were about to step out into a car park, stretching and checking the time on our phones. Everyone except me. And Lily. I didn't dare move.

What if we're not going where they think we are? What if this container is going to a dump? An incinerator? Or on the back of a truck, bound for a place to shoot us, starve us to death, sell us into slavery? It happens all the time. This could be what happened to Anya. A container, like this, the final moments of not knowing, being lifted through the air, to her death.

I thought about Jake. I was crying, too, now. It was all my fault. All of it. Whatever happened to Anya, Dima, me - it was all my doing. *I didn't save her. I made Dima come with me. I decided to go on this ridiculous journey. No-one else.*

Mum and Dad will go to pieces. The second of their children to die. At least they were prepared for Benji. You've tortured them, Emma. This past few months. Now you're going to die and one day they'll find out, or maybe they never will and you'll be missing forever, and it will destroy them.

We were jolted from side to side again, then crashed down. I felt my teeth rattle in my jaw as we landed. We all looked over at the same time, as the impact threw my hoodie from its place over Lily's face to the floor next to her arm. I couldn't handle seeing her. After everything, that's what sent me over the edge. I felt my heart race faster and faster, every breath get shorter and closer together. Stars appeared in the borders of my vision, all around the edges, sparking into the centre. Everything stopped.

***

We watched the doors reverberate. They jolted towards us, then back. The banging stopped.

'Guys, you're gonna have to clear the way. They're rusted shut,' the voice called through.

Those of us who spoke English motioned to the others to back up. I stood up, knowing I had to move Lily, trying to gather the nerve to do it. *Breathe.*

Dima stood up. 'It's okay,' he said, 'I'll do it.'

I exhaled and turned away, thumbing the tears from the corners of my eyes.

'You guys outta the way?' the voice called.

His voice was friendly. Definitely American. That was when I let myself believe we might be in the right place. I turned back and saw that Lily was with the rest of us.

'Yes,' Dima replied.

I watched him as the buzzsaw screamed, sending

171

sparks of orange sliding down the line where the doors met. It stopped. I looked at the seal. I held my breath. Another bang. Something bigger, heavier than before.

The doors cracked. Shards of metal clattered to the floor. A shaft of light appeared.

'Nearly in!' he called through the gap. I saw the bottom of his face. He had a hipster-style waxed moustache and a tattoo on his neck that made me want to cry with relief. Things that people who weren't fighting for survival had the time and energy for. I felt like I was closer to the world I left, back in the UK.

The final crash came straight through and the doors swung open. White light, the kind you get from fluorescent strip lights in supermarkets, flooded in. The man with the moustache slid the eye shield up to rest on his helmet. He took a step back, putting his sleeve over his nose. For a second, he looked at us, horrified. Then he cleared his throat, dropped his hand and forced a smile.

'How you all doing? Not good, I bet.'

His eyes rested on her body.

'Is that-'

'She's dead,' Dima said, 'she died on the journey.'

The man put the sleeved hand back over his nose and mumbled something. He motioned for us to step out onto the concrete floor. We did, slowly, carefully. I felt as though I had forgotten how to walk. Someone stumbled and had to lean on the man next to him for support.

The world outside the container felt too big. I needed shelter.

'Guys,' he called behind him.

We were in a hanger, or a warehouse, of some kind. More men in overalls joined him. They talked in hushed tones. Behind them I could see queues of people, lined up in front of a row of desks. To the right, chain-link walls that formed separate areas, containing people sat on benches. It all reminded me of the assessment tent at Calais. *Better resourced. More efficient. Could Anya be here?*

'This is New America, isn't it?' asked the man who quoted the statue poem to us.

The man who had broken through the doors turned around, taking his helmet off.

'Yes. It is,' he replied.

A buzz rippled through everyone. Everyone except me. I was watching the people in cages. I was watching his expression too - the man who got the doors open. He was nervous. People around me started to cry. Relief. Joy. Happy tears. They smiled at me and I tried to smile back.

'We're here,' Dima said to me, sniffing, grinning, 'I told you we'd make it.'

I opened my mouth to reply but I hesitated, not knowing what to say.

'My name is Andy,' the man with the moustache said, 'we have translators here, could you tell them?' he asked Dima, who relayed the information.

'Thank you,' Andy said, 'please tell them that we need as much information as they can give us, plus any kind of identification they have. Border security are on their way, with the police, to interview you all.'

'What do you mean? Security? Police?' Dima asked, frowning.

'You've arrived here illegally. You don't necessarily have a right to be here. Someone has died. There are procedures,' Andy said, motioning to his colleagues. They walked towards us, opening sets of handcuffs.

'No!' shouted Dima.

They stopped.

'Put it down,' Andy said, holding his hand out, 'put it down.'

I turned to see Dima, holding a jagged piece of metal

to his throat, from the smashed door. His teeth were clenched, breathing hard through them as he pushed the blade against his skin. His eyes scared me.

'Dima-'

'Don't!' he shouted, looking at me, then back to Andy.

The men carried on handcuffing the others, as though nothing was happening. They weren't even watching. It was just me, Andy and Dima who stayed still, a triangle of taut sides. *Fight, flight or freeze.* I froze. Again. My heart was rattling against my ribs but I could barely blink. I just stood there, staring at him, terrified the blade would pierce his skin.

'I. Am. A. Void.'

His voice cracked as he said those four words. It wasn't the coming of tears that cracked his voice, though. It was rage. The others were led away. I glanced at their faces as they left. Their tears were different. Not joy, relief. They were the same tears we cried when we were on our backs and the men were on the beach. They were the tears of the woman who tried to keep her bag, before she was shot. The tears of the man who protested his newly determined Void status, before he was wrestled to the floor and hooded.

All of them were crying. Except one. The man who had faith before still had faith now. He still had the same expression he did when he read that poem to us. I could see what he was thinking. This was all just a formality. They will do right by us. He knew it. He believed it and would continue to do so, until the end.

'Okay,' said Andy, holding his hand out, 'I hear you,' he continued, stepping forwards, 'I'm going to need you to-'

'Back off!' Dima shouted, thrusting the metal towards Andy, a quick jab in the air before sticking it

174

back up against his throat. I couldn't stand seeing his flesh bend, under the blade.

'Dima you can't do this, it's not worth this-' I started.

'Not *worth* it?! Is *my life* worth nothing?' he shouted, his eyes boring a hole right through me.

'Of course it-'

'It's your fault I'm here, Emma!' he shouted, tears finally filling his eyes. 'Your fault,' he repeated, almost whispering.

'I'm a Void,' he hissed through his teeth, looking back to Andy. 'I'm a Void, and the only place I can live, is here. New America. I got here. I *got here*. You have to take me. You have to keep me, otherwise I'm dead, do you see?' he asked, starting to laugh, tears still falling. 'I'm dead. So I might as well skip to the end if not, you see?'

His laughter melted into sobs. Just for a second, though. He kept control, taking deep breaths and planting his feet. He wiped the tears off his face with his free arm.

'Listen, man-' Andy started, then stopped.

We both ran towards Dima as the metal stuck in. I was screaming something, I don't know what. He was, too. I remember seeing his knuckles blanche, first of all. The effort of pushing it through his skin, down through the wall of his throat, dragging it across. I remember the blood was so dark against his skin. Almost black. He'd become so pale.

Andy got to him before I did. He pulled Dima's arm away, sending blood spraying out into our faces. At the time, I didn't register it. I felt it, and I must have known what it was, but I just ran through it. It was nothing more than the spray of an orange, when you peel it.

I struggle with that feeling, now.

I don't remember seeing the wound. I just remember

the feel of it. I pressed palms down onto it, as hard as I could against the hot, raw flesh, to stop the gushing.

'Give me your top!' I shouted at Andy. 'I can't move my hands and we need to pack the wound, give me your fucking top!'

He hesitated, then dropped the metal to the floor, pulled his t-shirt over his head and threw it at me. I stuffed it over the wound as fast as I could. Dima was choking. He was looking at me, but he couldn't talk. His body was shaking. Fitting, almost. I was kneeling next to him, I could feel his arm against my leg, trembling. I was talking to him. Telling him it would be okay and he would be fine, knowing it was a lie, while he stared back at me.

There was a rush of people around us. Alarms. Running. Someone appeared in my eyeline. A woman, a paramedic.

'What's his name?' she asked me, taking his pulse.

'Dima,' I said, 'it's Dima.'

'Okay. You've done a great job, sweetie, alright? We'll take it from here, okay? My colleague Ralph is going to take over on that wound for you alright, sweetie.'

A man's hands appeared over mine, waiting to replace them. I looked around to see him kneeling by me, impatient. I let go and shuffled backwards.

'He's going to be okay, isn't he?' I asked, suddenly sobbing. 'It's my fault, you see, it's my fault—'

'We're doing everything we can, honey, he's going to come to the hospital and we'll do everything we can for him, okay?' she said, not taking her eyes off what she was doing.

It all happened too fast. He was on a stretcher, then he was gone. It was just Andy and I left standing there, covered in blood, him without a top, me without my passport.

He still had it. *They'll find it.*

'No,' Andy said, holding his hand up to the man approaching me with handcuffs. 'I'll sort this one out. She needs medical attention.'

The man melted away. The hall carried on. Queues of people moved forward one at a time. Shouts of *next* in various languages echoed around. The people in cages coughed and cried, paced and panicked.

Some of them stared at us to begin with - a shirtless government worker and a dishevelled girl, both covered in blood - but they'd seen what happened. They knew it was just collateral damage. The story wasn't here. It was in the hospital.

'How can I find out what's happened to him?' I asked, staring at the doorway they had wheeled him out through.

'I'm not sure... there will be a way. I'll try.'

'Thank you,' I said, looking at him for the first time since I'd ordered him to give me his T-shirt.

He looked sheepish. Like he wanted to say something to me but couldn't. He took off his glasses and wiped his face with the back of his arm. *Is he crying?* He dragged his knuckles over his eyelids and sniffed.

'I'm sorry,' he said, 'I'm a good guy, you know. I'm not like one of them,' he nodded towards someone sat at one of the processing desks. 'For what it's worth,' he continued, 'some of you guys will get to stay, you know. Some of you will. But we're not the place people think we are.'

'What about Dima? If he... if he survives, I mean.' My eyes filled up with tears again.

'I don't know,' he replied, putting his glasses back on, 'I mean, he's a Void. That can go one of two ways.'

I shook my head, overwhelmed by the tears for a

few seconds.

'So after all this, he might be sent back, to the people who will kill him?'

I realised I was laughing. The same kind of laughing that came from Dima, before he stabbed himself.

'This is insane,' I said, 'it's actually insane. How can it be right? How?'

'It's best not to think about it,' he said, shaking his head, 'honestly. Even here, where we don't have the Worker Scheme, we're 'pro-migration', we take asylum seekers... we can still treat people like shit. We still just turn them away, when it suits us.'

'He's got my passport,' I said, looking at the doorway again.

'Has he? Hang on-' he frowned, fixing me with a sudden stare, as though I'd just dropped from the sky,

'what... what the hell - how did you- you're British, right?'

I nodded.

'I don't get it. You're not a Worker. You're not a Refugee. You're sure as hell not a Void. This doesn't make any sense.'

He looked at me again, from my feet up to the top of my head.

'You a journalist?' he asked, looking at my hands, then my face. 'Like, a student journalist or something?'

'No. I'm fifteen.'

'Shit. I thought you looked young.'

He took a deep breath and exhaled slowly, loudly, resting his hands on his hips.

'That's fucked up,' he said, shaking his head, 'I mean, it really is. What did they want with you?'

'Who?'

'The smugglers.'

'They didn't, well-' I stopped, thinking of the back of

the lorry.

'Fucked up,' he repeated, 'well, we can contact your family now, let them know you're safe. Those guys, they're absolute dirtbags, you know. To kidnap a fifteen-year-old girl on holiday with her family, sell you into the market like that-'

'What? I wasn't kidnapped. I wasn't on holiday. What do you mean, *the market?*'

'Wait, so how are you here, then?'

I breathed in and out, closing my eyes for a second. I had to tell him everything. Of course I did. But I was exhausted. I couldn't remember the last thing I ate. The last sip of water felt like it had been days ago, even though I knew that couldn't be right. I hadn't slept in too long. My eyes felt like they were bleeding. My body couldn't stand any more, let alone walk. Talking was a luxury I couldn't afford.

'I'm a British citizen,' I said, sitting down on the floor, crossing my legs. 'He has my passport. My name is Emma Morgan and I want to go home.'

Chapter 16

The hospital reminded me of Benji. I wasn't in the kids' bit - I don't even know if there was a kids' bit - but the smell was the same. The light, too. That clinical, cold light that makes your skin look sallow. We spent so much time there, before he died. Mum basically lived there. Dad was there a lot. Jake and I spent as much of the evenings and weekends there as we could. The children's hospital was a strange place. The walls were covered in bright, colourful murals. There were toys everywhere, mobiles hanging from the ceilings, the curtains around the beds had cute animal characters on them. Everyone smiled and laughed a lot. There was no escaping reality, though.

The reality was that *that* was the bit of the hospital where the really ill children were. Most of them would get better enough to leave, even if they'd be back in and out for the rest of their lives, but some didn't. Some of them, like Benji, would be moved to the hospice eventually. We didn't know that for certain, then, but it's what everyone there worried about.

I hope the bright colours, fluffy bears and shiny toys helped Benji. I hope they helped Jake, too. I hope they made everything seem less scary. More fun. More normal. Just like me, mum, dad, though - they weren't blind to

everything else. Just like us, they knew when things were
going wrong. The alarms going off when a child down
the corridor crashed and all the staff ran to her. The
parents, clinging to each other, sobbing as quietly as they
could manage, around the corner from their toddler's
bed.

Benji had enough to deal with. He was in pain. Jake
could see it. I would watch his face, wincing when Benji
cried. I could see his dismay when Benji would leave his
food, because he knew it meant he wasn't well. We all felt
it. I feel like Jake had it worst, somehow, because people
treated him as though he didn't know what was
happening, but he did. Maybe he couldn't articulate it,
but he knew it. He felt it.

What do you think he's feeling now?

I hated myself. I hated myself for what I'd done to
them. To Jake, especially. I had too much time to think.
To begin with, they put me on a drip. I was dehydrated,
anaemic. My blood sugar and blood pressure were too
low. They gave me vitamins. Slowly got my eating back to
normal. My water infection had gone up to my kidneys,
so they gave me a lot of antibiotics, too. I asked the nurse
whether anyone else from the boat was in the same
hospital. They would need all this, just as much as me.
More. She said she couldn't tell me. I didn't know if
Dima was in this hospital, another hospital, a prison. A
morgue. Nobody could tell me anything.

They said they couldn't let me call home until they'd
done all their checks, negotiations, god knows what else.
I wasn't allowed to leave my room. They gave me my
own room, with a bathroom, so that they could keep an
eye on me.

I'd never missed my phone as much as I did then.
To hear the voices of my family, of course, but also to
reconnect with the world. I felt like I'd been in outer

space, for the longest time, and now I was back, everything was different. I was different. I was an alien. I didn't like having time to myself, either. Not anymore.

Before, when I was at home, Jake was always trailing round after me and I found it annoying. I used to wish he'd just leave me alone. But lying in that hospital bed, pacing around the same ten-by-twelve tile floor space, I'd have done anything to have him there. Or mum, or dad.

A phone would have been company, even if I couldn't make calls or message anyone. At least I could read the news. Check social media. Watch a film. There was no TV in the room. No radio. No books. One magazine about hairstyles and another about motorsports. That was it. I hated being alone with my thoughts. I kept the nurses talking. Tried to make them like me, so they wouldn't leave.

I asked for a pen and paper, so I could at least write to keep myself company. They gave it to me, but it solved nothing. Alone with my thoughts, again. Only now, I could give my thoughts colour and shape and all the intensity I was trying to subdue, by writing them down on paper. I wrote letters to people who would never get them. I wrote a letter to Aminah. Another to Desange. One to Lily. I kept crying. I couldn't stop. Eventually, one of the nurses decided I needed to see their mental health staff.

'I just want to go home,' I told the man, again and again.

All I could think of was being in my bed, and staying there, forever. Sometimes, Jake would be allowed to come in and talk to me when I wanted company. Mum and Dad would be allowed in, for different reasons, depending on my mood. I would only get up to go to the toilet. I would watch shit TV, eat shit food and sleep shit sleep. That would be my life. That's what I wanted. He understood, he said. My parents would come as soon as everything was in order. He couldn't answer my questions about why it was taking so long. All he could say was that our governments were different and wanted different things. They were trying to compromise.

'You've been through a lot,' he said one day, when he had come to talk me through my new medication. 'You need to rebuild yourself, once you've rested.'

'I've been resting all this time,' I said, shrugging then pointing down at the bed I was sat on. 'I can't rest any more. It's making me worse. I need to start the next bit. Rebuilding.'

'Okay. What do you think is the best way to do that?' he asked, noting something down on his clipboard.

'I need to know what has happened to my friends.'

'Friends?'

'Dima. Anya.'

'Hmm. Tell me about Anya.'

'Dima was helping me to find her. Anya was from before. From back home. She's the one I went to find.'

He nodded, silently, resting his fingers on his lips.

He doesn't believe me.

'Look, ask someone at the place where they process people. The place I came from. They can back me up. Dima came with me, on the ship. He tried to kill himself when they started arresting people-'

He held up a hand.

'I know. I know about Dima.'

'You do? Do you know if he survived?' I leaned forwards, feeling something shoot through my frame, for the first time in a long while. I swung my legs over the edge of the bed, ready to leap off.

'He's alive.'

I jumped down and looked around for something to put on my feet. I was buzzing. He was alive. He was alive and-

'It's Anya,' he said, fixing me with his eyes.

'What-' I said, stopping, 'she's not - did she die? Don't tell me she's dead,' I said, stuck where I stood.

'Anya's not real, is she?'

I couldn't process the words. I stood, brows knitted, blinking, lips pursed.

'...What?' was all I could eventually come up with.

'She's a figment of your imagination. Someone your subconscious has created, to-'

I laughed, holding my hand up.

'You're joking, right? You're kidding me?' I said.

I didn't let myself fully react, because it couldn't possibly be what he meant. He continued to watch me, completely serious, unmoved.

'She's real,' I began, 'she-'

'When you go through something so extreme, your perception can be radically altered, you can retreat into an-'

'No! She's not someone I made up after that crossing traumatised me- she's the whole reason I left the UK, the whole reason I got myself into the camp, the facility, the-'

'I'm not talking about your journey across the continent, Emma. Or across the sea. I'm talking about your brother.'

'What does any of this have to do with Jake?'

'Benjamin. Your brother who died. Benjamin. The death of your brother was a cataclysmic shock, for all of you. Especially for you, though. You were so close. And at your age, you're in a very vulnerable position...'

His voice drifted, then faded into a dim buzzing, like the sound you hear when speakers are turned up, but the music isn't playing.

No. This isn't happening. How can I prove she exists?

'Look,' I interrupted him, 'she made this for me.'
I thrust my arm forwards, bending my hand back to
highlight my wrist. I watched his eyes search my arm.

'What?' he asked.

'My bracelet, she made it for me. With her-'

I looked at my arm. Then the other. It wasn't there.
He cleared his throat and leaned forwards.

'I'm going to recommend that you are transferred to
our child and adolescent psychiatric unit…'

He carried on talking. I wasn't listening. I was
searching through the bedside cabinet, for my bracelet. It
meant so much to me. It was all I had of her. It might be
all I ever would have, if she could never be found. I
threw out the two magazines, the boxes of tablets, the
bag of cotton wool balls and the patient information
leaflets. I dragged the cabinet out to look behind it. Then
I got on my hands and knees to look under the bed.

'You're not going to find it, Emma,' I heard him say,
'because it doesn't exist.'

'No. You've taken it. You took it, when I came in
here. Where's my stuff? Where are my things? My
clothes. These aren't my clothes,' I said, looking down at
the jumper and jeans I was wearing. I didn't recognise
them.

'We've given you clothes because you didn't have
any. I don't know what happened to the things you were
wearing when you came in but having heard about the
circumstances, I should think they probably weren't
salvageable.'

I knew they would be covered in Dima's blood. I
saw him again, his white knuckles pushing the knife
down through the skin. His eyes. His mouth, trying to
talk.

'So you did take them, then. And the bracelet. Look,
maybe you don't know what happened to her, but I need

to know where Dima is, and what's going to happen to him. If you don't tell me,' I found myself saying, 'I'll do the same thing he did. I mean it.'

Did I mean it? I didn't know. I felt so small, so much like one of Jangles' mice. It seemed like the only way to get their attention. To show I meant it. To get them to understand.

He cleared his throat and noted something down. 'I'll do what I can, to get an update on Dima. Okay? In the meantime, threats to yourself and others put you very much in the category of the CAP Unit. You're not doing anything to convince me otherwise.'

'Threats to others? I'm not threatening anyone - what's the CAP Unit?'

Then I shook my head, realising this was just a distraction.

'Where is Anya? Where is she? You must know. Or you can find out, right? Dima said you'd be able to. He said if anyone could find her, it would be in New America. You can. Can't you?'

'Let's start with one thing at a time, okay?' he asked, taking off his glasses and putting them in his top pocket. He clicked his pen closed and stood up.

'Wait,' I said, holding my hand up, 'wait. Jake, Jake can tell you. You must be in contact with my family, right?'

'We're making contact, yes, but-'

'Then ask Jake. He can tell you all about Anya. Ask him.'

He sighed. 'Get some rest,' he said, 'I'm hoping to get you transferred tomorrow, okay?'

'He'll tell you. Ask him about the alien fruit. And when we pulled her tooth out. Ask him.'

He winced. I saw him wince. He said nothing, but I knew what he was thinking. *This is bad. Worse than I thought.'* I watched him leave. I saw him shaking his head as he closed the door.

You have to get out of here, I told myself, *before they lock you up. Find Dima. Run.*

Chapter 17

'What would you do, if it was you?' I asked the nurse who came to do my obs.

'Honey, don't drag me into this. It's above my paygrade.'

She ripped open the Velcro armband and released my arm.

'I mean it, though. If the person you loved was somewhere in this hospital, but you couldn't see them, what would you do?'

'This kid your boyfriend or something?'

'Yes,' I lied, 'we were childhood sweethearts. We're going to get engaged on my sixteenth birthday. He's already bought a ring.'

Jesus. Where did that come from?

'Aww,' she said, 'that's sweet. How did you meet?' She marked my blood pressure on the chart and put the thermometer in my ear.

'Through school,' I said, hoping she wouldn't ask anything else.

'I met my fiancé at school,' she said, then smiled at the thermometer as she read it. 'Ah. Young love,' she sighed.

'How long have you been together?' I asked, finding my route in.

'Thirty-four years. And they said it wouldn't last. Can you believe that?'

I did my best pathetic smile and tried to stare into her soul.

She looked at me. I could tell she was considering it.

'My parents don't like him,' I pushed, 'but they don't *know* him like I do. They don't like where he's from. He'd do anything for me. He treats me like a princess. But they don't care because they think he's not-'

'-good enough for you,' she said, with a knowing nod.

'Exactly.'

She looked at the glass in the door, then back at me. She lowered her voice.

'Give me thirty minutes,' she said, 'I'll see what I can do.'

***

She appeared at the glass and unlocked the door. I was ready to go. Getting ready didn't take long. They had my passport. There was nothing I could do about that. Now that my bracelet had gone, I had nothing I'd left home with. Absolutely nothing. I stuffed some paper and the pen they'd given me in my pocket, along with as many tablets as I could fit. I left the letters.

She looked around, then unlocked my door and leaned through as she opened it.

'Come on,' she whispered, beckoning with her hand. The corridor was empty.

'If anyone asks,' she said under her breath, 'you ran out while my back was turned. Okay? You gotta be back here in an hour, remember? If you're not, I'll report you missing.'

I nodded, overwhelmed with a sudden urge to hug

her.

'Thank you,' I said, instead.

'Go on!' she whispered. 'Three floors up, remember? The guard will be gone for the next fifteen minutes.'

I walked fast and didn't make eye-contact with anyone. I tried to ignore everything that reminded me of Benji and that time. The sounds, the smells. I couldn't go there. *Not now.* I hit the button for the lift and looked to either side of me. A janitor was mopping the floor to my right, someone in scrubs was walking down to the end of the corridor on my left. I watched the numbers count up on the screen above the lift. I could hear the air rushing up the shaft every time it travelled higher. I could hear the voice say 'doors opening... doors closing' each time it stopped.

Shit. What if someone in the lift recognises me? What if security are in there? The lift was on the floor below us. *Doors closing.* Woosh. Fuck. *Doors op-*

I walked fast, away from the lift doors, past the janitor and turned the corner. I stopped and listened at the door leading to the stairwell. Nothing. I opened it, looking around. I could hear voices, below. I took a step over to the handrail on the landing and peered down.

Two people were making their way down the stairs, away from me. *Okay. Up.*

I climbed as fast as I could, keeping my eyes on my hospital-slippered feet as they scuffed up each stone step, gripping the end of them with my toes to stop them falling off. I wondered if I might have been better in bare feet, but it would mark me out, surely. As I stepped on to the final landing someone burst through the exit door, shouting. I immediately turned back and started to make my way back down the stairs, hoping they hadn't seen me. Someone was with them. I realised they were shouting and laughing, recounting some anecdote to each other. I slowed down and pretended to be fixing a problem with my slipper. They overtook me, passing me by without a glance.

Back up.

His ward was open. I'm not sure why they bothered having a guard for him. He wasn't going anywhere. Still, he was handcuffed to the bed. Even in New America, even in a New American *hospital*, the difference between a Void and a UK citizen was clear. I got my own room, despite the fact there was nothing really wrong with me.

He didn't, even though he nearly died.

He shifted in his sleep. *Is it sleep? It must be. He wouldn't move if he were in a coma.* His neck was covered in a dressing and he was wearing an oxygen mask. There were wires reaching out from under the collar of his hospital gown, trailing across to the machines on either side of him.

What now?

I realised I had no idea what I was supposed to be doing. *Fifteen minutes, you have fifteen minutes. Do something.*

'You lost, miss?'

The man in the bed next to Dima asked me. I thought he looked about Dad's age. He had a kind face.

'No, sorry,' I said, 'I'm just visiting him,' I said, pointing at Dima.

'You've nothing to be sorry for, sweetheart. Visiting him, huh?' he grinned and tutted, shaking his head, 'been a naughty boy, that one! Don't know what he's done but they got police guarding him. Seems a bit crazy, don't you think? I mean, look at him!' he laughed.

Dima opened his eyes and looked at the man, languidly. He closed them again. I wanted to move, to step towards him, but I seemed to be stuck where I was. He opened his eyes again. They settled on me. They widened. He started to cough, trying to sit up. Finally my legs worked.

'No, don't,' I said, putting my hands on his arm, 'don't move, you can't yet, I don't think.'

He stopped, staring at me, then pulled his mask away.

'What happened?' he asked me. His voice was raspy, quiet. His face was so pale. Those dark shadows hadn't lightened at all.

I realised, we weren't going anywhere.

'You don't remember?'

'No,' he said, 'they won't tell me anything.'

Oh fuck. What do I say?

'They wouldn't tell me anything, either,' I said, stalling for time.

'Are you okay?' he asked.

'I'm fine. Completely fine. I-' I stopped, trying to find the right words. *I can't. I can't do it.*

'How did this happen?' he said, putting his hand to the dressing on his throat.

'I - I don't know,' I stammered, 'we got separated. I don't know,' I repeated, not knowing what else to say. Flashes of what happened came and went. I flinched, feeling the blood hit my face.

'What's wrong?' Dima asked.

'Nothing,' I said, 'I'm just glad you're okay. They're keeping me in a room a few floors down. I don't know what they're going to do with us.'

He was watching my face, very closely. Narrowing his eyes, as though he was searching for something.

'You had blood on your face,' he said, frowning, staring more intensely.

'I have to go,' I said, 'your guard will be back soon. I'll come back when I can.'

'Stay,' he said, 'please stay, I'm scared, I-'

'I have to go. If they catch me here we'll be in even

more trouble. It will be okay,' I said, squeezing his hand, 'they just have to keep us safe while they sort their paperwork out to make sure we are who we say we are, that's all. I think you had a fight...that's why they're guarding you.' The lies spilled out like vomit, fast and messy. 'That's how you got hurt. They need to make sure you're not going to kick off again, when you're better. Just behave yourself, yeah? We'll be okay if we do what they say. It's all just procedure. You're in New America now. Everything will be okay.'

He squeezed my hand again. He wanted to believe me. So did I.

Chapter 18

I stood in the stairwell.

You need to get back.

I didn't move, though. I couldn't move because I was suddenly stopped by a thought. The thought that this whole journey might have been based on nothing. On a delusion. Seeing Dima lying there, so broken, jolted me.

My memory of him with that metal shard was so vivid, so immediate, it made Anya seem hazy. A distant memory. *An illusion?* That's what they thought. An illusion. A delusion. I'd ignored it since the doctor suggested it. Completely dismissed it. It was preposterous. Utterly ridiculous. Of course Anya was real. She had plaited my hair. Taken things from me. Given things to me. I pulled her tooth out, for Christ's sake. Jake was there. He talked about her when we were at home. And yet...

I listened. Someone entered the stairwell on the floor below. Their footsteps, *ship-ship-ship-ship-ship*, were making their way up, not down, I was sure. I looked over the handrail. It was a man, walking up. He looked up, right at me. I should have bolted. Somewhere, anywhere. But I couldn't. I stood there, waiting. *Ship-ship-ship.*

I sat down. I don't know why. I just couldn't hold my weight anymore. It was more than that, though. I wanted to make myself smaller, somehow. As though he wouldn't see me - if I just backed up enough into the corner and shrank into myself. Nobody would see me, ever again. This would all be over.

I watched, as though I was an invisible observer. I watched the top of his head, then his face, then his body, rise above the steps, then stop. He knelt down. I saw his face come into view. He was talking, but I couldn't hear him. I just heard water. Water, rushing in my ears. He put his hand out, placed it on my shoulder, still talking. I flinched. He took it away, then stood up. I remember watching him, calling. Shouting, I think. Then I buried my head between my knees and shut my eyes.

***

White. The whiteness was what I felt, first. I blinked, trying to blink the blurriness away. Things sharpened up. White walls. White sheets. I looked down at my chest. A white gown. It was so clean. Everything smelled white. The curtain was blue, though, the one around the bed. Like those blue paper towels you get in toilets, to dry your hands with. A big, concertinaed blue paper hand towel, reaching all the way around the bed. White noise, too. I shook my head, batted my ears, to clear it. I listened.

'Yeah,' a voice was saying, a calm, female voice. American. 'Yeah. Okay. We will. No. Nothing yet.'

I watched the paper-towel curtain. Whoever was on the phone put it down then coughed. I heard papers shuffling. I could smell something floral, above the white. Perfume. It reminded me of someone. I couldn't place it, but it made me smile. The curtain swished to one side.

'Emma?' she said.

The woman wasn't in scrubs. She was wearing

regular clothes. No stethoscope. She did have a pager clipped to her waistband, though, and a clipboard in her hand. She was in her late twenties or early thirties, I guessed, with a messy bun and a creased shirt. I decided I liked her.

'How are you doing tonight?' she asked, sitting on the bed, searching my face. 'You look good. Are you back with us?' she asked.

'Yes,' I said, 'I think so. Where did I go?'

'Somewhere we couldn't reach you,' she said, with a half-smile, then put her hand on mine and added, 'but we can now.'

American. The fact she had an American accent meant something important, but I couldn't think what. I looked at the window but the curtains were shut. Something caught my eye as I looked over. Bruises. Bruises on my arm. Both arms.

'What happened?' I asked her.

Her face changed. It seemed so familiar, the expression that passed across it. Like I'd seen it before, or felt it before, at least. She took a deep breath and took her hand off mine.

'Do you know where you are?' she asked.

I shook my head.

'Hospital,' I ventured, 'it's a hospital. Lulworth General. Is it? What happened to me? Is Jake okay? Was he with me?' I sat up, ready to find him.

'You're in hospital, that's right. Jake is fine. He wasn't with you, no.'

I exhaled and let myself sit back.

'It's not *that* hospital, though,' she said, almost squinting to remember what I said, 'Lilforth?'

'Lulworth General.'

'That's it. No. You're not there. This is New Manhattan Presbyterian.'

196

'Manhattan?' I said, convinced I'd misheard her.

'New Manhattan.'

'What?'

Her pager bleeped. She looked at it and pushed a button.

'Listen, it's been a long day,' she said. 'You need to rest.'

'I'm sick of people telling me I need to-' I started, then felt the memories coming back to me, like driving rain. 'Rest,' I said, following the rabbit down the hole.

Flashes appeared, behind my eyelids, whenever I closed them. I held them shut. Then I opened them because I couldn't stand it. Everything I remembered made me want to cry, or vomit, or both. I could hear her, doing something, saying something, but I couldn't see her. My eyes were open, but the images wouldn't stop even then. The square of light, getting smaller and smaller in the top-left of my vision, behind the lorry driver's silhouette. Aminah's face when she shouted at me, that first time we met. Seeing Dima fall as the shots sang past him. The blood, seeping out across the sandy dirt, behind her head. The children's tiny hands, picking up the scraps of potato skin as their mum stood against the wall. Lily's eyes, in the truck. Her eyes, in the container. The skin over Dima's knuckles, whitening as he pushed the blade in.

'Help,' I found myself saying, 'help me.'

***

'I have some good news for you, Emma,' she said. Katie, her name was Katie. The one who told me I wasn't in Lulworth. She was my doctor. She was the one who took over where the other guy left off.

'Your parents are here.'

'What?' I sat up and shuffled towards the edge of the easy chair. I had the best one in the Day Room. At least, *I* thought it was the best one, because it had a view of the park outside, rather than the TV. The medication I was on slowed me down a little. Made everything foggy. Her news made me move, though. I looked around.

'Here?' I asked.

'In New America. They're not at the hospital, yet, security are still processing them. But they will be. Tomorrow.'

'Is Jake with them?' I asked, gripping the inside of my slippers with my toes.

'No, he stayed home. With your aunt, I think.'

Aunt sounded weird. She was Auntie Ange.

'Can I see them?'

'Yes. Of course. That's what they're coming for. They're taking you home, Emma.'

She smiled. I stared at her. *Home.* I could barely remember it. I tried to remember my bedroom. I could remember Jake and Benji's. I could remember the kitchen. The garden. Or at least, the view of it from above, when I scaled down the side of the house. The cat. I could remember Jangles, curled up on my bed, but I couldn't see the rest of the room.

Katie's perfume reminded me of home. She had been everything since they moved me. Everything I had in the box marked 'truth' in my mind, was all from her. I learned about everything that had happened, why it had happened, from her. I wouldn't believe anyone else. I trusted her.

I realised I didn't want to leave her. She was the only one who understood me. She was the one who helped me to understand what was going on in my head, and how it had made all this happen. I knew, after she helped me to see it. I knew.

'The first meeting with them,' she started, 'I'll be there. Just to help with anything you find difficult, or they find confusing, or-'

'-don't leave me,' I said, pulling my sleeves down over my knuckles, 'don't. Please.'

'Like I said,' she carried on, 'I'll be there. But the next one, it'll just be you guys. If everything goes okay, you can go home with them.'

'So you're coming with us, then?'

'No, Emma. I'm staying here.'

'Well I can't go, then, can I?'

I was confused. How did she expect me to go anywhere without her?

She cleared her throat and leaned forward slightly, making sure she had my eyeline.

'You don't need me at home, Emma. You have everyone you need there.'

'No, I don't, I-'

'We've done so much work, Emma, to get you to this point. You've come so far. Remember, you have to keep moving forwards. Yeah? We've talked about this. This is what we've been working towards. It's a good thing.'

I was crying. It must have been bad because I never cried on those meds.

'Come on,' she said, putting her hand on my shoulder, 'You want to see them, don't you?'

I nodded. Of course I did.

'And Jake? You miss Jake, don't you?'

'Yes,' I managed, letting out a sob at the same time.

'Well, then. You're in a good place right now. It's time to move on.'

'But how will I know?' I said, rubbing my sleeve over my cheeks.

'Know what?'

'What to believe? Who to trust? What to think…
I…' I trailed off, seeing a look pass over her face. A
glimmer of a wince. She saw that I had seen it, though,
and quickly composed herself again. She straightened her
back, put down her clipboard and made sure she had my
eye contact.

'Centre yourself,' she said.

Katie told me to do this, whenever she could see I
was in danger of getting tangled up. 'Bring it back,' she
would say, 'back to the soles of your feet. Feel their edges
on the floor. The weight in your heels and the balls of
your feet. The touch between your toes. Now feel the air
moving in, then out of your lungs. Your nose, your
throat. Concentrate on it coming and going…' sometimes
she would carry on, but mostly after a while all she did
was say *centre yourself* or *bring it back*, and I had what I
needed. I would do it and remember the truth.

The truth was, Anya was made of grief. Her hands,
the ones that plaited my hair and held the railings so tight
- they were just my grief, stretching out into something I
could recognise. A girl. My age. Her beautiful hair. Her
smile. They were like the tears you cry when there's
nothing left to say. If you could capture them, make them
into a human form. That was Anya. Katie helped me to
see that. Understand it.

Anya represented what I was scared of losing, after
Benji died. Her courage. Kindness. Humour. They were
all the things I wanted to cling to. To make sure I kept
and grew, in spite of it all.

Katie was the one who got through to me. *And yet*, I
would think, *Anya was so real*. So, incredibly real.

The fact that my mind had the power to conjure her,
out of the fire, was too much for me. Once I realised that
all of it - the tooth, the sketch, her argument with Mia,
the present she left us - it all only existed *in my mind* -

that's when I became terrified. What else could my mind do? Dima nearly died, twice. I was assaulted. I could have died, too. My parents, my brother, had been through so much. All because of my obsession with an illusion. What else was I capable of?

I kept thinking about how much worse it could have been. I could have put Jake in danger. Katie explained that Jake had gone along with it, this imaginary friend, because it was fun. Something we shared. Make-believe, like no other. How exciting. The sister you always tried to rope into your world of monsters and dragons and fairies was finally playing along, like she meant it. She was so good at it. You loved this new friend just as much as she did. You shared a secret friend that you snuck out to see together. You took her presents. You took her seriously.

Once this all became clear, I was left so scared of my own mind, I didn't want to be left alone with it. Katie protected me, I felt, from what it could do. She knew how it worked and why it did what it did. I knew nothing.

She tried to show me I could control it, but I didn't believe her. Besides, I didn't want the responsibility. If I had done all this, the first time, what would I do if it happened again? I didn't like to think about it. I couldn't.

If I had to leave Katie, I was leaving it all wide open. My breathing was back to normal, but I was staring at her, still, contemplating how on earth I could let her go.

'You will be okay,' she said, 'I wouldn't let them do this if I didn't think you could handle it, I promise.'

Who is *them*? What is *this*?

'I don't have a choice, do I?' I asked, pulling a few strands of hair out. Just two or three. I did it whenever I felt I needed to break the tension between my head and my heart. Always from the back of my skull, towards the bottom, where nobody would see. For a while, at least. Katie hadn't noticed, at any rate.

She sighed and looked out of the window.

'You don't. No.'

She said the words quietly. She sounded tired. 'But it's the right thing,' she added, her voice suddenly brightening.

I looked up. She was standing up, smiling at a man who was walking through the door. They shook hands.

'Frank. Good to meet you again. This is Emma,' she said, presenting me. *This is Emma.* There was a tone in her voice I didn't like. Something between exasperation, relief, almost a hint of an embarrassed laugh - as though she was handing over a broken-down car to a mechanic. He shook my hand and smiled. I looked at them both.

'What's going on?' I asked.

They exchanged glances.

'We have to give the hospital a report, back in England,' Katie said.

'Which hospital?'

'The one you'll be transferred to,' Frank answered, avoiding my eyes for a second, then looking up, to search my face.

'What?'

I felt as though my guts were being pulled out of me.

'It's only for a short time,' Katie said.

'You said I was going home – you said –'

'You are. To the UK. Your family will all be there. You just need to ease yourself back in. You've been through a lot.'

'I trusted you,' I said, fighting back the tears, 'you're the only person I could trust, and you've fucked me over!'

Frank started making notes. Katie just looked at me. She'd run out of things to say.

I wished I was on the run again. *Fuck Katie. Fuck everyone.*

Chapter 19

'I'm not leaving until you tell me what will happen to him.'

'Come on, don't be like that. Your parents are waiting to see you.'

'What's the point? I'm not going home with them, am I?'

'You will travel with them, they'll be with you all the way until –'

'Until they dump me in an asylum?'

'It's not an *asylum*. You know it's not. You've seen the brochure. It's nice.'

I could tell she was tired of me. She couldn't wait to get rid of me. We both knew she would, eventually, so I had to change tack.

'Look,' I said, 'I just need to know what's going to happen to him. He risked his life for me –'

'We've been through this before, Emma, that's not exactly–'

'Let me finish. He nearly died, twice, and it was *my fault*.'

I could see she wanted to disagree, but she left it. I'd already refused to go to the first scheduled meeting with my parents. The tiny bit of leverage I had was the flight. I knew it was booked, I knew missing it would cause all kinds of trouble. So that's all I had. I just had to walk the line carefully enough to make sure I didn't get dragged kicking and screaming.

The balance of power was delicate. They wanted me to come of my own free will. It was better for everyone if I did. But if I could just resist enough to find out about Dima, everything would seem less hopeless. That's what I told myself, anyway. I didn't dare think about what I'd do if it was bad news.

I could see her weighing up the risks. My dad used to use a phrase whenever I tried something like this – refusing to do what I was supposed to, unless I got what I wanted: *We do not negotiate with terrorists.* He would laugh as he said it, shaking his head. I never won.

'This is important,' Katie finally said, 'I need to know I can trust you. You trust me, don't you?'

'Yes,' I lied.

'I will make enquiries about Dima. But I will tell you the truth, and you might not like it. I need to know you can cope with it. Because if you can't, that won't stop you getting on that flight. The only difference is... the *way* you get on it. Do you understand me?'

I nodded.

'I can deal with it,' I said, 'I promise.'

That was a lie, too.

***

How long had it been since I saw him, handcuffed to that hospital bed? I had no idea. Weeks, months? I could tell, from the grounds outside, that we were in autumn. It was beautiful. Mad beautiful. Like someone had taken a picture of a park in autumn back at home, then put a filter on and slid across to maximum saturation. The reds, oranges, yellows in the leaves – even the green of the grass, still. It was almost too vibrant. The trees were bigger, taller, wider. I hadn't seen anything of this place, except the grounds of the hospital. You could tell everything was bigger and brighter here, though, just from that.

That day, I wasn't allowed out. They were going to keep me in one place until I got on that flight. I looked at my suitcase. There was no point in having one, really. They'd packed it for me. I had no stuff of my own. At least I wouldn't be turning up with nothing again, like I did here.

I looked at my face in the mirror. I still wasn't used to it. I'd gone for so long without anything to see my reflection in, I couldn't get used to it. I looked different. Tired, harsh, somehow. What my mum would call *drawn*.

I ran my finger along my jawline, then up across my cheekbones. Under my eyes. *Where are you going? What is going to happen to you?*

I heard the door open behind me and watched it in the mirror. *Katie. Dima. Fuck!*

I spun around, looking at her, then at him, then back to her. I needed her to tell me he was real.

'Dima's here,' she said, 'he's here.'

He smiled, held his hand up to wave *hello*, just like he did the first time we met.

I struggled to stay on my feet. I found my hands over my mouth and nose, catching sobs, taking the tears from my eyes down to my wrists, to soak into my sleeves.

He walked over and wrapped me in a hug. I grabbed on to him, to stop myself from sinking to the floor. I buried my face in his shoulder. I couldn't hold it in. I was crying so hard I couldn't hear what he was saying. He held on. I looked over his shoulder and saw Katie, using the back of her hand to smudge away a few of her own tears. She sniffed and smiled at me.

'Thank you,' I managed, finally lifting my face

enough to talk.

He smelled clean. Healthy, if a person can smell healthy. I don't know what I mean, exactly. You'd know, though, if you'd spent so long trapped in a small space with people who smelled sick, like I had.

Dima held my arms and stretched back, looking at me.

'How are you?' he asked, smiling.

I laughed, sitting on the bed. This was madness. Katie sat on a chair by the window, facing away from us. I could see she was smiling to herself, though.

'I'm okay,' I said, still laughing, 'I'm fine. How about you?'

He shook his head, smirking, just like he did when he found out how I'd got to Calais.

'I'm good,' he said, looking at me. 'Do you need a tissue?'

I was covered in snot. I knew I was ugly when I cried. That kind of thing used to bother me. It didn't, now. I laughed and reached for the box on the bedside table, grabbing a handful.

'Jesus Christ,' I said, then blew my nose and cleaned up as best as I could. I gripped the damp ball of tissue and took a second to enjoy being able to breathe through my nose again.

'How's your...' I started, looking at the scarf around his neck.

He pulled it down. The scar was deep. Brutal. It had healed, but it was still angry.

We said nothing.

'I'm a citizen,' he said, finally.

'What?' I straightened up.

He smiled, nodding.

'Yep,' he said.

'Of New America?'

'It's all official. I'm not a Void. I'm not a Worker. I'm not a refugee. I'm a citizen of *New America*.'

He said the last line slowly, letting each word sink in, for both of us.

'Oh my god,' I said, not knowing how to react, 'wait –' I looked over at Katie, 'you're not lying, are you? You've not told him to say this, to get me to leave? To stop me breaking down? Are you both lying to me? Because I –'

'We're not lying, Emma, I promise,' she said, smiling, 'I wouldn't do that to you.'

'I'm not a good actor, Emma,' Dima said, shaking his head, 'and I couldn't lie about this even if I wanted to.'

I felt like I was floating. Nothing had prepared me for this. *Something good has happened. I helped to make it happen. I think.* For once, I hadn't caused suffering. Since his family was taken from him, Dima had only ever wanted one thing. He needed it, otherwise there was no point in being alive. Now he had it. Had I helped? Maybe. *Maybe I can feel something other than regret, now.* Something other than remorse. I could stop berating myself. Just a little.

I could do it, now. I could hold my fingertips against the string on the wall and follow it, back out of the labyrinth.

***

I sat down at my desk to write to Dima. They told me I wouldn't get my phone back until I was out of treatment. I had no idea what that meant. *Once I'd left this hospital, or the one in the UK? Not until I was off medication?* I didn't like to think about just how long it could take. *Once we're both back online*, I told myself, *everything will be better*. It didn't make me feel better, though, because I knew I wouldn't be in the same room as him for a long time. Maybe never. I felt heavy. Knowing I'd never feel the way I did that time when he kissed me, ever again. That perfect moment was just thrown away so quickly, trampled into the mud of everything that came after. It was only now that I could let myself think about it. Think about what we lost.

I stared outside and reached around to the patch at the back of my head, pulling strands with one hand, clicking and unclicking my pen with the other. I was privileged, to have a biro. Katie trusted me not to hurt myself with it, finally. I had to give it back in an hour though - she couldn't risk it getting into someone else's hands. *Come on, you're wasting time.*

Dear Dima

I winced and scribbled it out. Screwed up the paper.

Dima
I don't really know what to write. I just wanted to say

I didn't *know* what I wanted to say. I started to pull strands out from the fine hair just behind my ear. *What do you want to say?*

I kept thinking about his family. What had happened to them? What happened to him, after.

I wanted to tell you

Stop, I told myself, *stop it*. I was following the rabbit down the hole, tearing myself up, over what I had done to him. *You can't think about that.* About what he went through, on the journey. Or about what could have happened. *All that matters is he made it. He's a citizen of New America.* I looked out of the window, at the skyline beyond the park. It was like a caricature of a city. Like one of those prints mum bought for the living room when she redecorated to make it 'modern'. Elegant, ugly, dirty and gleaming all at the same time.

'Give me your tired, your poor,
Your huddled masses yearning to breathe free,
The wretched refuse of your teeming shore.
Send these, the homeless, tempest-tost to me'
Dima
I want you to know how much I

I rubbed my eyes and swore.

This is useless. I put down the pen and walked over to the window.

Dima I said in my head, looking at the red canopy of leaves and the concrete arms stretching to the sky behind them. *I was so angry with you, blamed you, for what happened to me… what nearly happened to me. I had to blame someone. I'm not past it, yet, but I still love you.*

I think I loved you before I even knew what colour your eyes were. When I saw you, asleep. I just didn't know it. I was obsessed with Anya. She came first. Or finding her came first, anyway.

Even after that night outside the medical tent, I still only wanted to find her. I wanted you with me, but I told myself it was for practical reasons, nothing more. Of course I needed you regardless. I wouldn't have got to Turkey without you. But I never let myself think about you in that way, after Calais, because I knew it would throw me off course. I had to be ruthless. And here I am, at the end of it all, and I know now that she was a lie. She was an illusion, a delusion, dreamt up from feverish grief.

I should have just let myself love you. I could have just loved you.

I watched the sky change from white to the purple-powder-blue haze that hung over the city when day turned to night. The air between my face and the window was cold enough to create a fine mist, blooming over the glass.

'Are you finished?' Katie asked as she opened my door. I turned to see her glance at the biro, the empty page, then me.

'Yes,' I replied, 'I am.'

***

I breathed them in.

Now I knew why Katie's perfume reminded me of home. It was the same as mum's. Of course it was. We stayed in one huddled mass, hugging, crying, for a long time. I wasn't crying in the same way as before, though. Not like when I saw Dima. I knew this was coming. I'd been expecting it. I think really I was crying because *they* were. And because I knew I'd hurt them.

I just kept telling them I was sorry. There was nothing else I could say.

'It doesn't matter,' dad would reply.

'You've nothing to be sorry for,' mum kept repeating.

That wasn't true. We all knew it wasn't. But I let her say it. Dad let her say it because she had to.

'Is Jake okay?' I asked, scared to look at them.

They both pulled away at the same time. I felt as though my heart had stopped, like it was waiting for the answer before it could continue beating. They were wiping their faces, straightening their clothes. I held my breath. *I can't stand this.*

'He was very, very upset, Emma,' mum said, looking at the floor.

'You've been gone for three months,' Dad took over, 'it was a long time for all of us. But he's only a child. Remember how long summers seemed when you were his age?' he asked.

'But he's okay, isn't he? He's not...'

'Damaged?' Mum said, suddenly fixing my eyes.

Yes, that's exactly what I meant. I just didn't want to say it. I looked back at her.

'I don't know,' she said, finally, 'We don't know. We have to hope not, don't we?'

We stood in silence. *Centre yourself. Bring it back.*

We didn't talk, beyond the basic necessities, all the way back. In the taxi, the airport, on the plane. I couldn't talk to them. They couldn't talk to me.

Katie hugged me, before I got in the cab. Wished me luck. Told me to stay in touch. I said I would, knowing I wouldn't. I had to leave her behind, properly. Forget her. Mum and Dad said the odd word to each other. *Where are the documents? Wait here while I go to the toilet. You need to eat something.* They talked to me in tiny fragments. *Are you cold? Try to sleep. Take this, come here, have a sit down.* The silence between us grew.

I tried to sleep on the plane. At least if I closed my eyes and shut myself out of the present, we all wouldn't feel the emptiness so much. That's what I told myself. I hoped they would talk properly, to each other, while I listened, if they thought I was really asleep. They didn't.

In the queue after we landed, I read the banner across the wall. *UK Border Force: Protecting Us All.* I watched the queue on the opposite side. People who had come from all over the world, hoping to be accepted into the Worker Scheme. Who would get to a Worker Camp? Who would be sent back, who would go to Calais, Turkey, who would try to make the crossing to New America?

Who would live?

Who would die?

'Emma!' I heard my dad shout. I realised I'd been holding our queue up. He was waiting in front of the desk. My passport was in his hand. I walked over and watched the guard as he took it, looking at me, then the photo page. Again and again. I looked nothing like her, that girl in the photo, anymore. He typed on his computer. Held the photo page over a panel that scanned it. Looked at me again. His computer beeped. He read something, hit a key. Then he handed it back, without looking up. I took it and walked through.

I gripped the little burgundy book. My passport was the one thing that had made it all the way with me, except for when the hospital had it. Battered. Stained, water-damaged, dog-eared – but it was still with me. I thought about the people in the queue, on the other side. The man who was wrestled to the ground in the Assessment Tent in Calais. The woman who tried to get her bag back, outside the Facility in Turkey. Lily, in the container. None of them had a little burgundy book. *Neither does Anya,* a voice in my head said. *No. Stop.*

I took a deep breath, while we waited by the carousel. I tried to feel the tip of each toe against the inside of my trainers. The inside of the arch of my foot against my sock. *Bring it back.*

***

The unit was just like the brochure. Credit to them, they didn't oversell it. The Formica, lino, polyester was exactly the same in real life as it was on the photos.

I still hadn't seen Jake. They thought it would upset him too much. Upset me too much. *I* thought it would kill me if I didn't see him soon. This whole time he was the one person I hadn't let myself think about, because he meant too much. Now I was no distance from him, but I couldn't see him. He was my brother. My living brother. He'd been so mixed up in all this, before I left, too. I needed to see him, to get past it.

They told me I wouldn't be there for long. I had to adjust to the new medication. Work on being out and about, back in the normal world. Going to the shop. Making a cup of tea. Feeding the ducks in the park. We actually did that, as though I was five years old. They kept talking about school. I was supposed to be doing exams, in the spring, but I might have to repeat the year.

We'll see, they said.

I just wanted to see Jake.

I thought, *maybe if I do everything they ask me to, I might get out faster.* So I did it. I talked bullshit in therapy. I took my medication. I accepted the little challenges, completed them, without rebellion.

I couldn't let myself think about what I would do when I got out. The future. Where I would go, who I would see, what I would do. I just focussed on seeing Jake again. Maybe he needed help, like I did. I couldn't bear to think of him needing anything and not getting it. I didn't like to think about my parents. They visited, but every time they turned up without Jake, I just felt like shit again.

I didn't have a *Katie* in the unit. There was no bonding with anyone. Turnover was too high. It was okay, though, I didn't need her anymore. I could do it on my own. I could. I would.

I had a sort-of friend, though. Charlie. In the room next to mine. She had her own problems, lots of them- but she always had time for me. Always made me laugh. She had a lot of scars, and a bald patch everyone could see, unlike mine. Mine was still hidden. I tried to stop it growing. Hers got bigger and bigger. Right at the front of her parting. It wasn't just from pulling hair, though, it

was from the damage she did by hitting her head on the
wall. I hated hearing it, but I never told her I had.

'What *the fuck* is that?' she asked when we were in my
room.

We were looking through my sketchbook. Drawing
was one of the activities they encouraged me to do. They
thought it was therapeutic. I laughed.

'It's supposed to be a power plant.'

'A what?'

'My dad works at one. A power station. You know,
with the cooling towers,' I pointed at the looming
shadows, rising above the smaller structures.

'Why would you draw that?' she asked, frowning.

'I don't know. Just something I grew up with, I
suppose. It's always been there, in the background.'

She flipped through the pages. 'Woah,' she stopped,
flattening her hand over the paper, letting her fingers slip
down the pencil lines.

We both stared at it.

It was Lily. Her face. Her eyes, looking over at me. I
drew her, again and again, because I knew she was real. I
knew she had been there, with all of us, with me. I knew
she wasn't with us anymore. But she *had* been. Nobody
could tell me she hadn't.

Charlie didn't ask who she was, why she looked the
way she did, anything. She just stared at it. I think she
could tell that it was one of those things we wouldn't talk
about. We never talked about why we were there, what
had happened to us, what our problems were. We had a
kind of silent understanding. We pretended none of it
was there, none of it had ever been there. It never would
be there, again.

She closed the sketchbook and looked around,
sighing.

'You really should unpack, Emma,' she said, her eyes

resting on my suitcase. It was still on the desk, exactly where dad left it when he dropped me off.

'There's no point,' I said. 'I'll be out of here soon.'

Charlie didn't answer.

Chapter 20

I sat in the visitor's lounge, waiting for mum and dad. They always came to see me on a Sunday. I think we all found it depressing. I started to wish they wouldn't come.

I let my fingers creep up to the nape of my neck, where the hair was missing. I felt around for the edge of the patch and grabbed on to the strands that bordered it. I pulled a couple out. Just enough to take the edge off.

'Emmy!' I heard his voice and looked up. *Jake*. It was Jake.

'Jake!' I jumped up and kneeled down, opening my arms as he ran towards me. He was laughing. He grabbed me and clung on as I picked him up, squeezing him close.

'You've grown!' I said, letting some happy tears fall before fighting the rest of it back, for his sake.

'I have!' he replied, 'it's on the wall at home, you can come see it!'

'She can,' mum interrupted, 'when she comes home, but she's not coming home just yet. It'll still be there, though, you can show her then.'

I looked at mum and dad and wondered what had made them bring him.

'When will you be coming home?' Jake asked. His eyes were so close to mine and they were so earnest, I could hardly look at him.

'Soon,' I said, 'really soon, I hope. I'm so glad you

came to see me!' I said, trying to sound bright.

'Jangles got run over!' he blurted out.

'What?'

'She's fine,' Dad said, sounding irritated already.

'No she's not,' said Jake, 'she lost a leg! It's so cool. You should see her, she's –'

'– Emma doesn't need to hear about the cat, Jake,' Dad said, 'tell her about your new class.'

Jake looked crestfallen.

'Come on,' I said, 'let's sit down and you can tell me about your new class at school.'

I squeezed him and sat him on my knee. I didn't want to let him go.

We talked about his new class. Who he sat next to, the class hamster he wanted to bring home for half term. Mum and dad watched us. I think they looked happy. I think. For the first time since… well, I couldn't remember the last time I thought they looked happy. Maybe happy is too much. Relieved, maybe. Reassured. Some kind of weight was lifting, at any rate. They were smiling. Mum reached over and held dad's hand.

Dr Kendal appeared in the doorway and watched us for a moment, before walking over.

'Mr and Mrs Morgan,' he said, holding out his hand.

They shook hands and said hello.

'Thank you for coming in,' he carried on, 'shall we go next door?'

This was news to me. I thought they were just here to visit. They looked nervous again, glancing at Jake, then me.

'He's fine here,' I said, 'what do you think I'm going to do? Jesus Christ I'm not going to kidnap him, okay?' I snapped.

'Jake is fine to stay here with Emma,' said Dr Kendal, holding his hand towards the door, shepherding them out.

They left.

'So what happened to Jangles, then?' I asked as soon as they were out of sight.

Jake's face lit up.

'She managed to get out even though mum was keeping her in, and she must have walked for ages and ages because we got a call from a vet all the way up in Todbrook, and it was late at night and they said someone had brought her in in a washing-up tub because they didn't have a cat carrier or a box and she couldn't walk or anything and there was blood coming from her nose and her back leg was all wonky and – and they had to do an X-ray and it was broken in too many places to fix so… so they asked us if we wanted her to die or not and mum said no so they said they'd take off her leg instead as long as we could pay for it.'

'Wow. Poor Jangles. Can she walk yet?'

'Yeah. She wobbles a bit and she can't seem to get her jumps right yet. When she tries to jump from the sofa to the windowsill she misses. I think Mum's happy though because it means she *has* to be an indoor cat now. Or that's what Mum decided anyway. Dad says the vet *didn't* say that but that's only because he doesn't like having the litter tray. Mum says she doesn't know why he cares because it's not like it's him that cleans it out anyway…'

I smiled. I did want to go home. I missed it.

'Did you find Anya?' Jake asked.

I felt a wave of nausea rising up my torso, into my throat. I held my hand over my mouth and willed it to pass, closing my eyes. *Breathe. Bring it back.*

'No,' I said, 'no I didn't.'

Breathe.

'Oh no,' he said, 'where is she then? Did she die?'

218

'I… I don't know.'

I watched the doorway, willing them to appear.

'Dad told me we'd imagined her. But we didn't, did we? She was real, wasn't she? She was our friend.'

'She wasn't real, Jake,' I managed, 'I made her up. Because I was upset, and I needed a friend. You could see her in your mind, like when we play the castle game.'

A layer of sweat had spread over my neck and lower back. My eye twitched and I rubbed it furiously to get it to stop. 'She's like the knight, or the jester. We see her, but no-one else can. But she's gone now, anyway, because that game has ended. We'll find a new one, when I come home.'

I exhaled. Jake frowned. I could see cogs whirring in his brain.

'Come on, Jake,' Dad said, from the doorway, 'we need to get going.'

He was smiling. Mum appeared. She was smiling, too.

'Emma,' she said, 'we'd better get your things together.'

'What? What do you mean?'

'You can come with us. Dr Kendal just discharged you.'

Jake squealed and started running circuits around the chairs and tables.

'Are you serious?' I asked, feeling suddenly wired.

'Yep,' Dad said, 'look, we've got your massive bag of drugs, so we're all set.'

He held up a plastic bag full of boxes of my prescription pills, grinning.

Fuck. I didn't know whether to laugh or cry. I did both.

***

My bedroom. Jesus. There was my bed, just as it had been the morning I left. The rest of the room, that I couldn't remember when I was in hospital, took some getting used to. I felt like it was different, somehow. Had they painted it? Changed the curtains? I looked at the bookcase. I didn't recognise the spines. Were they new? None of the titles, the colours, the fonts, looked like my books. I took a step closer and reached out, tracing my finger across them. I picked one out. The font was swirly. It looked like fancy joined up handwriting, but the letters were at jaunty angles. *Confessions of a teenage shopaholic.* A stylised illustration of a girl with her arms full of department-store bags, walking down the street in high-heeled boots, followed by a tiny dog in a jumper, stared back at me. This was definitely not my book. I put it back. None of them were.

I looked at the wall. That was another difference. I could see the marks where my posters and photos had been taken down. The walls were bare. I knew there had been posters. Postcards. Photographs. All over, it looked like, from the traces of sticky marks, the faded edges where the sun had bleached around them. What were they, though? I couldn't remember.

I was sure my medication had messed up my memory, although they told me that wasn't a side effect they often saw.

I exhaled and sat on the edge of my bed. Everyone was downstairs. Mum and Dad made Jake leave me alone, for a little bit at least, while I unpacked. He was grumpy, but I promised him I would take him to the swings when I'd finished, which made him cheer up.

My door creaked.

'Jangles!'

She was purring so loudly it sounded like a

lawnmower. She'd lost weight. She wiggled through the gap and head-butted my leg, rubbing her body against my calf.

'Wow, look at you,' I whispered, watching the space where her back leg had been. The fur was growing back, but there was still a big square around the wound, like the patch Charlie had on her scalp. I put my hand to the one at the back of my head, to reassure myself mine was smaller.

'Oh Jangles, I missed you. We've both been in the wars, haven't we?'

She smiled with her eyes and purred. She always smiled at me like that.

My eyes rested on my suitcase.

'Okay, let's do this. Start putting some of myself back in this room, hey?'

None of it was my stuff, of course, but at least I had my drawings. I could put *them* up on the walls, at least. Nothing scary, though, I didn't want anything up there that might upset Jake. Just the nice stuff.

I pulled out the clothes that New Manhattan Presbyterian had given me, my sketchbook and my bag of toiletries. I noticed a crumpling sound, like a plastic bag, from the black fabric lining the case. I felt it. There was a bag in there. I swept my hand to the edge and found a zip. Undoing it, I felt with my other hand.

Clothes, I thought. Clothes for washing? Had they separated my stuff out for me? I pulled back the panel and the white plastic bag sat there, staring back at me. I could already see what it was. The blood stains showed through the thin white film. It was the clothes I was brought to the first hospital in. The ones I'd been searching for, that they told me must have gone.

I stared back at it, feeling my chest thud. I slowly got to my feet and closed the door, quietly. I glanced at

Jangles. She stretched out on the bed, curling her paw into a contented hook over her nose. *Breathe. In through your nose, out through your mouth*, I told myself. *Slow it down. Bring it back.*

My fingers were shaking so much. I fumbled with the layers, grabbing the clothes lightly, as though I would feel what happened when I last wore them, just by touching them. I was right, though. I flinched, feeling the blood hit my face again. Walking through the spray. *Did it go in my eyes?* I felt like I could remember seeing red, blurring over my field of vision, but that was probably a false memory. Probably. Katie had told me about those. I put the pile of clothes on my knee.

The t-shirt, soaked with his blood, was on top. My fingers hovered over it. I could smell the metallic, sour smell of blood. Or maybe I just *thought* I could. It smelled real, but Katie had told me how powerful the mind was. What trauma does to you. I blew slowly out of my mouth and managed to drag the stained top over to my left, onto the floor. The harem pants were underneath. They didn't have as much blood on them, but they made me feel more nauseous. All I could think of was when they were pulled down, on the back of the truck. Feeling the air around me, seeing my own blood run down my legs. My body hitting the road, pulling them up, looking at the sky.

I couldn't touch them. I just couldn't bring myself to do it. Instead I stood up, letting them fall to the floor. Jangles was watching over the edge of the bed, interested in the string tie dangling from the waistband. I wanted to vomit, at the thought of her going near them. I backed up against the windowsill and tried to focus on the pads of my fingertips, touching the cold glossed wood. Jangles jumped down. *Please don't.* Her tail swished. I turned and pulled up the sash window, leaning out to retch. It was a dry retch. *Keep it together*, I told myself. *Keep it together.* The cold air rushed in and helped me breathe. Helped me see. I pulled myself back inside and straightened up, closing my eyes, letting the head-swim subside.

I could hear her behind me, skittering around the room, making the strings dance for her, like she did with mice. I swallowed and turned around. It wasn't the strings. It was something else. Part of the drawstring had broken off, maybe. But it was a different colour. It was red. White. I took a couple of steps forward as she rolled onto her back, grabbing it between her front paws and kicking it up with her back legs. She tossed it across the floor and flipped back over, tail swishing, thinking about how best to attack it next. *Fuck.* I lunged, scooping her up. She struggled against me but I held her firm and opened the door, breathing hard, depositing the wriggling fur-bag on the other side. I closed it before she could scoot back in.

It was over there, lying on the floor, in the corner. It was waiting for me. My hands were behind my back, still clinging to the door handle. I let go, letting my hands slide down the door and rest at my sides. My chest was thudding again. *Come on.* I willed my feet forwards. The walk across was only five steps. It seemed to take years. I dropped to my knees, knowing exactly what was in front of me. I opened my mouth, reaching my fingertip up into the back of it. I felt each tooth. I knew they would all be there, but I had to check. No gaps. None missing. The only person missing a tooth was Anya.

It was there, on my floor, crossed with red cotton from her cardigan. Two plaits of thread reached out on either side, one scratched button at one end, a loop-tie frayed almost to breaking point at the other, just as it was when I last wore it. I picked it up, held it to the light, examined each groove in the tooth, felt the points of the

roots. I held it between my palms and breathed, closing
my eyes, feeling my pulse return.

Chapter 21

'I don't think you should take Jake out, not right now,' mum said, looking out of the front window.

'What? Why?!' cried Jake, running over to peer over the windowsill.

'I promised him,' I said, zipping up my coat.

'Who are they?' Jake asked.

I looked out. There were maybe a dozen people, with cameras, microphones, watching the house. One of them saw us looking out and smiled. He turned and said something to his camera man then started walking up the path.

'Shit,' said Mum, pulling the curtains together.

We heard the knock at the door and looked at each other.

'Who are they?' Jake repeated.

I went into the hall and looked at his outline through the frosted glass of the door.

'Don't answer it!' Mum hissed.

'We're not prisoners in our own house, Mum. Come on, Jake, we're going.'

Jake ran to grab my hand, grinning.

'Don't take him, at least, Emma, please-'

I'd already opened the door. I closed it behind us before she could say anything else.

The man's questions were drowned out by the

clamour. They seemed to move as one body with lots of legs, scuttling up the drive, cameras flashing, shouting questions in our direction. For a second I stopped, but as they crowded round us I decided to carry on, dragging Jake along. They were too close. I picked up Jake to carry him and it gave one of them the chance to get right in my face.

'How do you feel, Emma, about what you put your parents through?'

Then another.

'What did you see in the Turkish facility? Is it true that they beat people?'

I faltered. Jake was heavy. He was getting scared, I could tell from the way he was gripping my arm. The swings were half a mile down the road. Mum was right.

'Emma,' I heard a voice, from the back of the crowd, 'Emma, Emma I'm sorry-' she struggled through the bodies to the front. The journalist from the Herald.

'I'm so sorry,' she said, 'it's Jen, we met before you left, I was the one who said Anya would be in Calais. I never thought you'd- but I'm just so glad you're okay.' She had tears in her eyes.

'Emmy, I want to go home,' Jake said, putting his head on my shoulder.

'Do you have a car here?' I asked her. She nodded.

'Give me five minutes. I need to take Jake back first, but I want to talk to you.'

***

Her house was a mess, and I loved it. I knew my house would be exactly the same, if I had one of my own one day. Books, papers, pot plants, coats, shoes, mugs everywhere. There were at least three cats. One in the hall, one in the living room and another the kitchen. I hoped there were more upstairs. The place smelled like toast and coffee.

'I'm so sorry about the mess,' she said, filling up the kettle. 'I wasn't expecting anyone.'

I shook my head and smiled, stroking the kitchen cat. He was a grey and silver tabby, with slightly longer, tuftier fur than Jangles.

'Don't be, it's a lovely place.'

She watched me while she waited for the kettle to boil. I could tell she wanted to ask me what happened but didn't know where to start. I decided to tell her what I'd come for.

'I need your help,' I said, 'I need to find out if she's alive or not. I've just got a new phone and I've been searching through loads of-'

'-she's alive,' Jen interrupted me, 'that's what I wanted to tell you, but I couldn't, in front of them - the press. Nobody knew about her because your parents never told the media you'd gone to find her. They just said you'd gone to volunteer and you'd-'

'-She's alive?' I interrupted, 'How do you know?' I managed to get the question out before the tears took over. I was laughing and sobbing at the same time. The kitchen cat jumped up and sat on my lap, as though it knew I needed a cuddle. I stroked it with one hand and soaked up the tears with my jumper sleeve of my other arm.

'I've been researching the Lulworth story since the fire. Then you went missing, and there was the campaign to find you - everyone was suddenly interested. All they knew was that you'd visited the camp, though. You were angry about how the authorities handled the fire. About the Worker Scheme in general. They didn't know about Anya.'

'How do you know her name?'

'Someone leaked the records to me. It took a lot of doing. She was the only fourteen-year-old girl there. Why didn't your parents talk about her, in the campaign?'

I shook my head, staring at the grain of the wooden kitchen table, trying to figure it out.

'I suppose…' I started, 'I never told them her name. But they knew I'd made a friend there, that's why they grounded me. But then… it was quite a while after the fire, that I left. And I pretended everything was fine, in the meantime. Tried to make them think I was over it. I never talked about her. Maybe they thought I'd just gone to join the cause.'

Jen nodded. 'The media did,' she said, gripping the empty mugs.

'And then… they convinced me… the doctors, that she wasn't real. That I'd imagined her.'

'Why?'

'I've been asking myself the same thing. I don't know what came from the doctors and what came from my parents but that's what they all believe. It's what they made *me* believe, too. But then I found her bracelet and I knew my instinct must be right, even after all this time.'

She put my mug of tea in front of me and sat on the chair opposite. 'Have you thought about what they might gain from painting you as an unreliable witness?'

I didn't know what she meant. I shook my head.

'What else did they tell you?' she asked.

'Nothing, really… other than Katie. I asked her to find out about a boy I travelled with. I met him in Calais, Dima. He came with my to Turkey, then on the ship to New America, too.'

'What happened to him?'

'He's a citizen, now,' I said, smiling, 'he was a Void, you see, and-'

'How did you meet him? In fact, just tell me, from

the beginning, in your own time. I want to know everything. I want to tell your story to the world, if you'll let me. I think it needs to be heard.'

I felt caffeinated. That same feeling I had when we were sailing around the cove to the harbour, where the shipping containers waited. It felt good, this time, though. Like I could use the energy for something important. Something urgent.

'I need to know about Anya, first,' I said, realising my voice was trembling a little.

'Of course. Do you want to speak to her?'

I shifted forwards suddenly, making kitchen cat jump off my knee.

'Seriously? How? Of course I do!' I was nearly shouting.

She smiled, reaching for her phone.

'She's not in this country. But she's safe, she has a home, she's not in the Worker Scheme anymore.'

I tried to process the words as she tapped and swiped her phone screen.

'I don't understand, how-'

'We'll do a video call, shall we?' she asked, smiling.

I was shaking, grinning, crying, all of it. She could see what it meant to me.

'Just remember this, when the big-shot journos want you to themselves, yeah?'

'Of course, of course,' I repeated, hardly able to get the words out.

'And I want an interview with Dima,' she added, 'that will really make it. I don't know anyone from the UK who has managed to interview a resettled Void. It's so rare.'

'I promise. He'll want to talk to you. He sent me photos of him with his foster family, he said he's starting school, I-'

I stopped as Jen turned the phone screen round to face me. I watched my blotchy face laugh as the ringtone sounded, then my face shrank into the corner of the screen and was replaced by Anya's.

'Anya!' I shouted.

'Hello Emma! Jen told me she'd call if she managed to talk to you, I'm so happy to see you!' she said.

I stopped for a second, taking in her face. She had scars, new scars, all over one side of it, down her neck. One of her eyes looked cloudy.

'This is from the fire,' she said, pointing exactly where I was staring, 'but don't worry, I'm fine.'

'I'm sorry, I didn't mean to stare, I just, I didn't know-'

'When did they find you?' she interrupted me.

I was grateful.

'Once I got to New America. Where are you?'

The room she stood in gave nothing away. There was a bookcase behind her, but I couldn't make out the titles.

'Germany. Berlin.'

'Berlin? You're kidding.'

She looked confused.

'No,' she said, 'they have a sanctuary scheme here, it's-'

'Sorry, I should explain. Berlin was the place my school trip was going to, the one I pretended to be on, but I wasn't, and - well, I'll tell you all about it. First though, how are you? How did you get there? Look, I found your bracelet!'

I held my arm up, brandishing my wrist, holding her white tooth and red cotton braids up to the camera. She couldn't believe it.

Jen set the phone against her empty mug and smiled as we started to tell each other everything.

'Hang on,' she interjected, 'do you mind if I record this?'

'Please do,' I said, 'like you said, it's a story that needs to be told.'